COVEN
OF THE WITCH

BY HEATHER G. HARRIS

PUBLISHED BY HELLHOUND PRESS LIMITED

HELLHOUND
PRESS

For my awesome supporters on Patreon, with special mention to Amanda Peterman and Melissa. I am so grateful and humbled by your belief in me.

I am so thankful to my two amazing ARC teams. Thank you for all you do for me, I swear I never take it for granted.

My newly formed Audiobook ARC team have hit the ground running, helping me get some reviews on all of my beautiful audiobooks narrated excellently by Alyse Gibbs. I want to thank them for all their hard work and for all those hours of listening. You guys have blown me away with your enthusiasm. Thank you to both teams, you make me feel like I'm not alone in this endeavour.

Final mention to my dear friend Lisa Heiser who is just such a wonderful human. I am so grateful for you.

Content Warnings

Please see the full content warnings on Heather's website https://heathergharris.com/content-warning/ if you are concerned about triggers.

The Other Witch series has scenes which reference dementia, mental illness, attempted suicide and suicide. Infrequent poor language is used.

Please note that all of Heather's works are written in British English with British phrases, spellings and grammar being utilised throughout. If you think you have found a typo, please do let Heather know at heathergharrisauthor @gmail.com. Thank you.

Chapter 1

'Her sweet, loving nature will be remembered and sorely missed.' I ended my eulogy.

There wasn't a dry eye in the house. I had managed to hold it together, though I'd needed to pause a number of times. Hopefully people thought it was for dramatic emphasis rather than because I was getting choked up. Nobody would expect me to choke up over a familiar, especially when I didn't have one of my own.

The small body rolled forward into the cremator that we kept in our basement. As witches, we use the fiery machine entirely too frequently, mostly to get rid of black magic and dark objects but sometimes bodies, too.

There were wails of sorrow as Cindy rolled forward in her little wooden box. She had been Meredith's familiar and, though she was just a cat, the whole coven grieved. Familiars are sacred and sacrosanct and her death had sent shockwaves through us all. Something within us had fractured and friends huddled together, eyeing other groups with open suspicion. They knew that *someone* amongst them was a black witch. And someone *had* been … but she had swallowed a deadly potion rather than face my justice. Now the teenager lay in a coma.

Ria had made bad choices but she didn't deserve to die for them; she was still a kid. I was going to save her and then I was going to hunt down the witches who had targeted her and led her astray, who had preyed on her inferiority complex and her need to belong. Them, I would happily see dead.

I cleared my throat, drawing all eyes to me – and then I lied. 'I am pleased to confirm that our suspicions about a black witch operating out of this coven have proven unfounded. A third party has been found, turned over to the authorities and will be duly punished.'

'Who was it?' Melrose demanded, surging forward. 'Who killed our Cindy?'

I didn't have the faintest clue but it hadn't been Ria. I had another black witch to find still nestled in my coven. 'I'm not at liberty to divulge that information whilst the prosecution is ongoing,' I said instead. 'Rest assured, justice will be meted out. A wake will be held for Cindy in the coven common room for those who would like to attend.'

My words did the trick and I watched as tension drained out of people's shoulders and eye contact and timid smiles started to appear. I couldn't have my coven divided; divided we were weak but united we stood a chance against the darkness lurking within. Besides, this way the black witch would let down their guard. They would think I'd arrested someone else, an outsider. They would be mistaken and I would be waiting.

There hadn't been one black witch in my coven, there had been two: a full witch and an acolyte. Ria was the acolyte so she was accounted for, but her mentor – who had slaughtered Cindy – was still not accounted for. There was a slight chance that an outsider had managed to get into the coven to carry out the murder, but it made far more sense that it was someone from within. Occam's razor: the most likely explanation is probably the right one.

The killer was someone who knew that Meredith had an open-home policy and her door would be unlocked. They'd slipped into her home, gutted her familiar and slipped away again undetected. No, as much as I wanted it to be an unknown third party, it was more likely that someone in my coven was a black witch dealing in pain and death. And I would find them.

The wake was a sombre affair. Normally at wakes you can tell funny or heart-warming stories about the deceased, but we didn't have that option with Cindy. There were only so many times you could recall her purr and how she'd loved to curl her tail around our legs. Someone told a story about her bringing in a mouse when she was a kitten, but that was it.

Melrose made a beeline for me. 'Where is Merry?' she demanded harshly. 'Ria and Meredith would never miss the ceremony for Cindy. Where the hell are they?'

'They're having a holiday,' I lied again. I was getting good at it. 'Meredith couldn't face seeing Cindy cremated.'

'Bullshit.' Melrose wagged an angry finger in my face. 'She would have sobbed her heart out but she would have been here. I don't believe you, Coven Mother.' She spat my title like it was an insult.

I smiled serenely. 'You don't need to believe me, Melrose. The truth is the truth.' And a lie is a lie.

I'm not usually a fan of lying. My friend, Jinx, is a human lie-detector and I know she hates it when you lie to her. I did my best not to and it had been somewhat habit forming – but there was a time and place for everything.

I couldn't let the coven know that Ria was sick, and I couldn't let the black witch that lurked amongst us know that she had tried to kill herself rather than remain in the malevolent black coven.

Melrose glared at me, shook her head in disbelief and turned to stalk away. Bastion reached out and grabbed her shoulder. 'People are grieving,' he said softly. 'Spreading rumours and hatred in a time of grief is reprehensible.' His voice was gentle but his words were not. Nor were his eyes: he fixed her with a glare and they flashed yellow in warning. Suddenly his pheromones filled the air and his presence as a deadly predator was overwhelming.

Melrose swallowed hard, her hands suddenly shaking. She'd gotten the message loud and clear. *Keep your suspicions to yourself or else...* She spun around and walked away; significantly less stable than she had been a minute before. I watched as she gave Venice a wan smile before excusing herself from the wake.

I met Kassandra's eyes across the room and jerked my head towards the exit. She nodded and made her way out, leaving her assistant Becky talking to the new wizard, Edward. I met Kassandra on the stairway, Bastion trailing behind me. Even though my ORAL potion was complete, the coven Council in their wisdom thought it best that he

7

still guard me until such time as another witch managed to replicate the complex brewing process. If I were the only one who could do it, they'd keep me chained to a cauldron for the foreseeable future and I didn't want that at all. Luckily, I was sure that at least a handful of witches up and down the country had the skills to replicate the potion.

My patent had been processed and a usage license drawn up. I would earn fifteen percent of every single potion sale. I had deliberately kept my percentage small because I wanted the potion to be as widely available as possible. The higher my percentage, the more the sellers would drive up their prices to make whatever baseline profit they were aiming for.

I'm not greedy, and I had plenty of other patents earning me an income. The whole point of the potion was for it to be accessible to everyone who needed it. The only problem was obtaining the ingredients, some of which were really rare. I was working on securing a sustainable supply line, though.

By unspoken agreement, Kassandra and I held our silence until we were in my coven office. The silence was mournful and respectful, both of us lost in our own thoughts, mired with grief. The loss of a familiar was incredibly rare and it cut far deeper than I'd expected. The silence felt fragile, and I didn't want to be the one to break it. I gestured for Kassandra to take the guest chair – covered with low-level truth runes – whilst Bastion took up position by the door, a silent sentinel who missed nothing.

'A sad day,' Kassandra finally commented. 'A murder of a familiar...' She trailed off and reached up to touch Jax, her bearded dragon, which was resting on her shoulder. He leaned into her touch and they shared a moment that I would never have.

I am the only witch I have ever heard of without a familiar. That I had no soul was one of the common refrains of my childhood, and you can only hear a thing so many times before you start to believe it. Something must be deficient in me for me to have no familiar but, whatever it is, I am determined to overcome it. I will succeed and prove all my naysayers wrong. With the ORAL potion, I was halfway there and my name was firmly on the map. Now all I needed was a production line and the potion would change lives everywhere. Familiar or not, I was going to make history.

'A very sad day,' I agreed evenly.

'You've found the culprit?' She asked the question but her tone was cynical; she hadn't believed my lie. Was that because *she* was the culprit? Or was there another reason?

I studied her. 'Not exactly,' I admitted finally. 'I found a black witch but she was an acolyte. She wasn't the one that killed Cindy.'

'Ria,' Kassandra surmised. 'You've turned her and Meredith over to the Connection?'

'Meredith is with her, but Ria has not been arrested,' I word-smithed neatly. Not technically a lie at all. Omission is my best friend.

Looking grave, Kassandra nodded then steepled her fingers. 'But we still have another black witch to deal with, the one that killed Cindy.'

'Yes, I think so, but they may not be situated here.' I hesitated. I wasn't sure how welcome this observation would be, but she still needed to know and I wanted to see what she would do with the information. 'When I was in Liverpool, there was some evidence to suggest the black witch was operating out of *your* coven.'

'My coven?' she said incredulously. She sat back into the chair, dumbfounded. 'I've never seen the slightest hint that there's a black witch operating out of Liverpool.'

'Your stores were missing a significant volume of hydration potions, and we both know what that means.' It meant that someone within her coven was regularly practising bloodletting. Bloodletting itself isn't necessarily a black-witch art, but utilising it regularly and hiding it certainly suggests that someone was doing something nefarious.

Kassandra looked dismayed. 'How did you find out?' she asked, trying to regain her composure.

'Jasmine. I was injured when I did some potion-ingredient retrieval with Bastion. He took me back to your coven for healing. Jasmine healed me but I'd lost some blood so she got me a hydration potion. She said that she doesn't often go to the potion store herself, but this time she did and she immediately noted the missing vials.'

Kassandra rubbed a hand over her face. 'Goddess, this is a mess. Two black witches, operating out of two covens?'

'You've never suspected that a black witch is in your coven?' I asked again, watching her closely to see if she looked uncomfortable whilst the truth runes worked their magic on her.

She shook her head. 'No, never. I honestly thought I ran a tight ship.' She grimaced. No doubt, like me, she was thinking how badly this would reflect on her when it came out.

I studied her. She might be my rival for the position of witch member of the Symposium but I believed her.

Which was a pain in the ass because I really had been hoping that she was the black witch.

Now I was back to square one.

Chapter 2

Although I had tried to persuade Kassandra that the black witch was in her coven rather than mine, I knew that wasn't necessarily true. Before Ria had swallowed her deadly poison, she'd told me that there was a black coven. Black witches were scattered up and down the United Kingdom, but they all belonged to one black coven. It was worse than I'd feared; not only were there other black witches in existence but they were working together. They were organised, they had a power structure – and evidently they had an agenda.

With black witches littered everywhere, I didn't know who I could trust. Ria had said that there was even a black witch on the coven Council. I had limited resources and even fewer allies.

I was leaning towards believing that Kassandra was one of the good ones. Even knowing about the black coven's existence was dangerous so, instead of telling her about it, I had simply given her the incentive to find the black witch that was lurking in her own coven whilst I dealt with my own.

'I think that under the circumstances it's best that you return to Liverpool,' I suggested.

She smiled ruefully. 'You just can't wait to get rid of me, can you?'

I hesitated. 'It's not been unpleasant having you here,' I finally admitted. 'Having someone take over a lot of the organisational duties and the teaching has freed me for other pursuits. But now that I've finished my potion, I think your presence in your own coven would have greater value.' That was surprisingly diplomatic for me.

'Hunting my own black witch?'

'Exactly.'

She nodded briskly, 'Fine. I will file the paperwork to the coven Council notifying them of my return.' She studied me. 'If you don't mind a little unsolicited advice?'

I gave a sharp nod for her to continue, even though unasked-for advice is right up there on my list of pet peeves. If I want help I'll ask for it, but in this instance curiosity got the better of me. I wanted to know what she thought I was doing wrong.

Kassandra rubbed her wrists with a grimace. She caught me looking, set her hands back on her knees and cleared her throat to bring my attention back to her face. 'If you'd delegated a little more to Ethan, Jacob and Jeb, you wouldn't have needed a temporary Coven Mother.'

I pinched my lips together but I knew that she was right. I'm a control freak, but if I was ever going to become a Symposium member, I would have to learn delegation – and it would have to start now.

'What's up with your wrists?' I asked sharply, instead of acknowledging the advice.

'I have a condition,' she said shortly.

'What sort of a condition?' I pried.

'A private one.' She stood. 'I'll get my things packed and Becky and I will be out of your hair within the hour.'

Becky was her assistant who trailed along after her glaring at me. She seemed to have taken Kassandra's appointment as my temporary Coven Mother as some sort of insult. Some people in life always find an issue even where there is none, and I guessed Becky was one of those types. I'd be glad to see the back of her, though if I were honest I would miss Kassandra's efficiency. It rivalled my own. Although sharing the role had been hard, she had made day-to-day life significantly easier. Obviously, I said none of that. Kassandra shut the door behind her, and the moment was gone.

Bastion turned to me as if he was going to say something but my phone blared to life. I held up one finger in a 'just one moment' sign and answered the call.

It was Dick Symes, the water elemental. 'Miss DeLea, you owe me two favours.' He wasted no time getting straight to the point, which was one of his few characteristics that I actually liked.

'Two favours to be called within three months' time. No injury, harm or death to befall anyone as a direct consequence of those favours,' I noted.

'Yes, yes,' he said impatiently. 'I need you to come to my residence. Right now. Be discreet.' He hung up without securing my agreement and that set my teeth on edge. I wasn't an acolyte to be summoned with a click of his fingers. Still, I did owe him and I would prefer that the favours be discharged sooner rather than later. I texted Oscar to ask if he could drive me to the Symes' residence or if he'd had a drink or two at the wake. He responded immediately saying he was good to go.

Dick hadn't said what he wanted me to do, which made packing my bag tricky. I put an array of potions and a range of paintbrushes into my tote bag, then added my rune stones in case he wanted me to scry someone. If he needed anything else, he would have to wait for me to come back here to get it. That would serve him right for being a rude and impatient sod.

'Dick Symes is calling in his favour,' I explained to Bastion and he nodded.

Bastion is a griffin, and he is widely recognised as one of the deadliest assassins to walk this earth. Each magical species has their own cross to bear; for the griffins, it is a powerful urge to kill. If the urge were left unchecked it would lead to a massacre, so the Connection, the ruling body of the Other Realm, had allowed the griffins to form a guild of assassins. The guild allows them to work out their deadly urges in a measured way, including by accepting paid contracts from the government.

Bastion had once taken a contract on the love of my life, Jake. Someone had been trying to kill Jake for some time but he'd survived through my judicious use of my sentient family grimoire, Grimmy, and some less than savoury spells I'd found therein. I'd brought Jake back to life, but I hadn't managed to save his sight or the roguish good looks of which he'd been so proud. To keep him alive I'd sequestered him in a remote house where he'd lived a half-life and grown more and more bitter as the years rolled by. I should have done more to help him but I'd been so obsessed with keeping him safe that I hadn't let him *live*. In the end that had killed him – but the responsibility for his actual death lay in Bastion's hands.

Bastion has a rare magical gift: he can coax. If you have the slightest inclination to do something, he can fan that tiny whim into action. He had made Jake kill himself by leaping from the top floor of our house. Jake must already have had the urge to die to allow Bastion to grow it – and I was the one who had put it there.

I'd let Jake down miserably and that would haunt me for the rest of my days.

Chapter 3

I fought the blush that was trying to rise. I was incredibly glad that Oscar, my driver and pseudo-father, wasn't in the room to hear this. 'You want me to do what?' It took an effort to keep my voice even.

Dick smirked at me, relishing my discomfort. He really was a dick. 'I have a lady friend in the parlour and I want you to paint a rune on me that will let me fuck her for hours. I don't have the staying power that I used to.' He leered at me.

'Isn't it a bit early to be getting it on?' It was only 6pm.

Dick snorted. 'Every hour is sexy hour if you're motivated enough.' He swung his hips around and did some thrusts like he was limbering up. Oh heck. I could never unsee that.

'Right, well, I'll need some skin—' I kept my tone business-like.

He started to drop his trousers and I whirled around so I wouldn't see any more. What I'd already seen would definitely scar me because Dick was going commando. 'No, no! Just your back will do,' I said hastily. 'Lift up your top.'

'Okay, I've taken my shirt off.'

Removing the shirt was as unnecessary as dropping his trousers because I only needed a small patch of skin for the runes. But I wanted to get it over and done with, so I turned around reluctantly. Thankfully, Dick had buttoned up his trousers; instead of flashing me his tackle, he was flashing me a lascivious smirk. I am all for body confidence but I sensed he was trying to make me feel as uncomfortable as possible. He appeared to be an exhibitionist and he seemed to consider this as part of his foreplay. It wasn't something I'd signed up for.

With a moue of distaste, I grabbed the potion I needed and quickly painted on *wunjo* for pleasure, *inguz* for seed and then *isa* to activate them.

'Now we're talking!' Dick chuckled as he visibly rose to the occasion. His slacks tented.

I hastily packed away the potions, not even bothering to clean my brush. 'Wipe the runes off your back to end it. If you leave them on for longer than a couple of hours, things are going to start hurting,' I said briskly. I grabbed my tote bag, slung it over my shoulder and hustled for the exit.

'My love,' I heard Dick crooning to his ladylove who was waiting in the parlour. 'I've got a present for you...'

Crikey. If that was what he thought constituted foreplay, I felt sorry for his companion. But then again, what did I know? It wasn't like I'd had *any* kind of play in years, fore or otherwise.

Bastion and I barrelled out of the house and slammed the door behind us before we could hear more. We paused in the night air and leaned against the wall.

'That was horrendous,' Bastion muttered. 'And I can't unsee it. At least you got to turn around – I had to keep eyes on him because he was a potential threat. I saw *everything.*'

'He was a threat to my mental health,' I complained. As one, we pushed away from the house and approached the car. 'Don't tell Oscar,' I entreated.

'Believe me, I don't want to talk about this ever again.' He shuddered a little.

I grinned as we climbed in the car. In the beginning I had hated Bastion's presence because having a guard had felt smothering and unnecessary, but now I found I rather enjoyed having a companion to share in the horrors of my day.

'That was quick,' Oscar commented.

'Hopefully not *that* quick after all that,' Bastion muttered.

I couldn't stop my little snicker but I quickly changed the topic. 'Can we go to The Spice Shoppe? I need to pick up some more ingredients.'

Oscar turned the car towards High Wycombe. The Spice Shoppe is run by John Melton from my coven, who professes to be a spice and herb specialist selling more than 2,500 products. For most people his shop is a source of great cooking ingredients, but for the local witches it is our apothecary. Here we can buy both mundane and rare potion ingredients, and lazier witches can purchase pre-made potions. I have little need for the latter because I prefer to brew my own. It isn't just a matter of trust but of excellence: my potions are better. Even so, we often purchase potions for the coven's store from here, especially when my time is limited.

We arrived fifteen minutes before the shop was due to close. I knew that John would stay open for me if I needed him to, but I tried to hustle around as quickly as I could. It wasn't fair on his employees if I made them stay late. I grabbed some ginkgo, rhodiola, hawthorn and echinacea for my personal stores; for the potion for Ria, I selected cranesbill, shepherd's purse, cinquefoil, witch hazel, goldenrod and yarrow. I lugged them over to the till where a grumpy looking employee scanned them. Even without the absence of the Other realm symbol on his forehead, I would have been able to tell that he was from the Common realm. Any Other realm employee would have been falling over themselves to make sure I was happy with their service; nobody wanted to piss off the Coven Mother.

The Common realmer rang up the bill. Did he not find it bizarre that people were willing to spend such vast amounts on herbs and spices? I paid, pleased that I'd managed to find everything I wanted and in record time, too.

John came over as I was packing the ingredients into a cardboard box. 'You have an excellent eye. You've picked out the finest specimens.'

'As always, there are only the finest specimens to be found here.' I returned the compliment to finish our well-worn dance.

'You're too kind, Coven Mother, too kind.' He bobbed his bow again and touched his hand to his heart. John couldn't possibly be the black witch in our coven simply because that required some original thinking and he

The fireball hit his feathers and there was a faint smell of burning. Griffins are resistant to flames but not impervious to them, and the stench told me that he was suffering. I looked up at his chiselled jaw but his blank face gave nothing away.

Bastion couldn't end the threat whilst he was protecting me so I reached into my skirt pocket, pulled out my emergency potion bomb and called a tendril of my magic forward to activate it. Bastion watched my movements with bright-yellow eagle eyes. He craned his head around to check the location of the fire elemental then gave a sharp nod. He knew what I was planning.

I popped my head quickly out of the protection of his wings, reached up and threw the potion bomb towards the fire elemental. I had intended it as a distraction to allow Bastion time to retaliate, but I wasn't the best at throwing. Instead of landing a few feet away as I wanted, it struck the elemental directly in the chest.

The bomb exploded in a wave of purple fire and heat. The flames were witch fire, nothing like the red flames that had danced on the fire elemental's head, and there was no chance he would absorb them. He started screaming just as the force of the explosion threw Bastion and me back into our car with a loud crunch. Dazed and confused, I lost a few seconds. My ears were ringing and my head was swimming. My chest hurt.

When the ringing in my ears stopped so had the elemental's screams; he had either escaped or he was dead. Given that he'd taken a potion bomb to the chest, I was betting on the latter. Guilt and remorse threatened to swamp me but he'd been trying to *kill* me. My guilt and remorse could take a long walk off a short pier. They had no place here.

Bastion unwrapped his charred wings from around me and shifted back into human form. His transformation was instant and, unlike a werewolf's shift, he had retained his clothes during the change. He was instantly dressed in black combat trousers and a black top so tight that it might have been painted on, showing hard, corded muscle underneath. Not that I was looking, of course. We were friends and friends don't notice each other's bodies, especially not at inopportune moments such as when their bodies have been flush against each other during an explosion. Nope, I didn't notice them at all. And why had his T-shirt gone in the partial shift but was back in the full shift? It was one of life's mysteries.

'Nice throw,' he complimented me, sounding impressed. The shift had healed the injuries that he'd sustained in the attack, but some of his blood was on the pavement. That indicated his injuries from the bomb were far more serious than I'd thought.

'I was aiming for the pavement in front of him,' I confessed, making Bastion grin.

He pulled me to standing and checked me over. 'You okay?'

'Fine.' I dusted myself down and winced as my fingers ghosted over my ribs. 'No lacerations, but I think I've broken a rib or two. You? Your wings must be wrecked.'

He shrugged it off. 'Nothing that the shift couldn't heal. I'm fine.'

I flicked my eyes over him. He was indeed *fine*. I turned to check on the damage to the car and gasped as I saw a familiar body on the ground next to it. 'Oscar!' I screamed. The driver's door was open and he was on the pavement, blood pooling around his head.

Bastion swore darkly as we both ran to him. I threw my ever-present tote bag on the floor and ripped out the potions and brushes stored there.

'He must have got out to help us and been hit by the car when it was rocked backwards by the force of the explosion,' Bastion surmised grimly. The explosion – and us. I wasn't all that weighty but Bastion was, and the explosion had flung us and the car backwards, straight into poor Oscar.

I hated how pale he looked. His grey hair was swept across his ashen skin and I could see all the lines that now adorned his face. Oscar was getting old. When had that happened? In my head he was still fifty and strong as an ox but he wasn't. Dammit, what had I been thinking still having him in the field with me? He was in his sixties. I had been abominably selfish.

I lifted up his shirt and hastily painted two runes onto his chest: *hagalaz* for injury and *sowilo* for health. I sent my magic through them and the cut on his head started to heal instantly. Despite the small pool around him, he couldn't have lost *that* much blood; head wounds always look worse than they are. At least the bleeding had stopped. My main concern now was brain damage and I prayed to the Goddess that, at most, the knock had merely concussed him.

'He's stable,' I said briskly to Bastion. 'But we need to get him to the tower so I can make a potion to help with any brain swelling. Can you put him in the back of the car – carefully – and I'll drive us to the tower.'

Bastion hesitated for a second. 'What?' I demanded impatiently.

'I need to check on the fire elemental.'

'Quickly, then!' I snapped.

'Fine – but heal your ribs while I do it,' he ordered.

'Fine!' I retorted. 'But hurry!'

I grimaced but obeyed his flinty-eyed command, pulled up my shirt and painted on some hasty runes. I pulled my magic towards me and let the runes light up. Healing yourself rather than someone else is harder because it requires a bigger pull of magic, but even so I was relieved when the pain faded. I hadn't realised how much it hurt until the pain had gone.

Bastion took me at my word and covered the distance between us and the fallen fire elemental faster than I would have thought possible. I could hear sirens screaming through the air in the distance. We needed to leave.

John hustled out of the shop. The cynical part of me thought that he had waited until the danger was over before stepping out. 'Are you okay, Coven Mother?' He was wringing his hands and looking pale. It was noticeable that he didn't spare a glance for Oscar who was lying on the ground in front of him. Not everyone liked having wizards in the coven, but I hadn't realised that John was one of them. Was the delay in him coming out mere cowardice on his part or something more sinister? Goddess, it was hard suspecting everyone and anyone of being a black witch.

'I'm fine,' I said calmly. 'The authorities will be here soon. Do the usual, please.'

John nodded briskly, happy to have a task. He hesitated as he turned to the shop and looked back at me. 'I was in the back room,' he said sharply. 'If I'd known you were being attacked, rest assured I would have been at your side. I'm glad you have your griffin. Keep him with you.'

Oddly, I found that I believed him. There were still good men and women out there; I was getting too cynical, too jaded. I scrubbed my tired eyes.

John gave me a little bow, which I barely reciprocated, then continued into the shop to do what was needed – wipe the security footage not just for his shop but all the surrounding cameras too.

I sent out a coven-wide text message: *Does anyone have brain-swelling potion in their personal stores? Positive replies only. ADL.* Brain-swelling potion isn't used regularly enough to be held in the coven's potion store – it doesn't keep well – but I had a faint hope that someone might have brewed it recently for a client. I couldn't recall seeing it in the client logs but maybe something had happened under Kassandra's reign that I didn't know about. If not, I'd be brewing it tonight instead of working on an experimental potion to save Ria from black mordis poisoning.

Bastion returned to the car looking grim. He opened the back door and gently laid Oscar on the seat, strapped him in with the seatbelts then climbed into the front passenger seat. Apparently I was driving us home; Bastion didn't like driving because it meant that his focus wasn't on me. I'd come to like that too, though I wouldn't admit it even to myself.

'The elemental?' I asked.

'Dead.'

I'd have time to examine how I felt about that when Oscar was okay. I said nothing, put the car into gear and drove off. Fear for Oscar was running through me and everything else was secondary.

He was going to be fine. He had to be.

Chapter 5

I was sweating over the small pewter cauldron. No one had responded to my text message and now I was brewing the brain-swelling potion myself. I flicked my gaze to the DeLea potion bible. I knew the brain-swelling potion like the back of my hand, but this was *Oscar*. So I had my textbook out, just to be sure. I followed Delilah DeLea's instructions to the letter.

I tested the temperature again before sliding in the last of the yarrow. I stirred the cauldron briskly, checking the temperature frequently and altering the flame as required. I kept my mind on the potion and not on the purple flames that had consumed the fire elemental at my behest. Not on Oscar, pale-faced and surrounded by a dark pool of his own blood.

The potion slowly turned yellow and I knew it was done. I turned off the flame and stirred it slowly to help it cool, then lifted the cauldron by its tripod chain and carried it to the waiting ice bath. Ignoring the ice's hiss of protest, I carefully placed it in the ice and stirred a little more vigorously. I tested the temperature again but it still wasn't cool enough to drink. Impatience clawed at me but I kept stirring; *patience is a virtue,* Mum's voice murmured in my memories. She was right; good things come to those who wait.

Fear gnawed at my gut but I obstinately ignored it. Nothing and nobody bossed me around, not even my baser instincts.

When the potion was cool, I decanted it into vials: one for Oscar, and nine more for our potions store. It had a very short shelf life but that was better than letting it go completely to waste. I marked the expiry date on the vials and made a note on my phone's calendar. If the vials still hadn't been used by that date, we'd take them to a hospital and a cross-over nurse/healing-witch who could give them away. Cross-overs are people who do the same job in the Common realm as they do in the magical one.

For the potion to work, the patient has to have some innate magic. There are a surprising number of Common realmers who have some minor latent magic – enough to spark the potion, if nothing else. It was better than pouring it down the drain, and maybe we could cause a few miraculous recoveries. We all deserve a miracle in our lives. Goddess knows, I prayed for one for my mum every day.

I carried the vial into my lounge where Oscar was lying unconscious on my sofa. 'He can be violent when startled,' I warned Bastion.

Bastion nodded like that made sense. 'I'll hold him down.'

I bit my lip; the feeling of being restrained would almost certainly exacerbate the problem if Oscar regained consciousness. I contemplated painting *isa* on him with some anaesthetic potion, but I didn't want to force him deeper into unconsciousness if I didn't need to. Perhaps it would be fine.

'Oscar,' I called, quietly at first then louder. He didn't respond and I grimaced. The hard way, then.

I opened his mouth, poured in the contents of the vial, then stroked his throat to make him swallow reflexively. He swallowed once but that wasn't enough for him to ingest all the potion. Before I could encourage him to swallow more, his eyes flew open in panic and he started to strain wildly against Bastion.

'Oscar!' I shouted, 'It's okay! It's Amber! I'm healing you. Calm down, you're okay!' His wild eyes gained some focus as they snapped on to me, but he still struggled against Bastion. 'Let him go!' I instructed sharply.

Bastion released him and moved back rapidly. Oscar surged to his feet, looking more than a little feral. His hand went into his pocket, pulled out a lighter and flicked a flame into life.

Tension hummed in the air. Bastion's muscles suddenly seemed even bigger than usual; he was taking up more space in the flat than he had done moments before. If Oscar used the IR – the intention and release – to grow the flames, he could do some serious damage.

I waved a hand at Bastion: *relax*. Oscar would never hurt me. 'Oscar,' I repeated, my tone gentler. 'You were hurt but you're okay now. Swallow that last bit of potion and you'll be fine,' I crooned softly.

He breathed heavily through his nose before looking at me. He didn't spit the potion out but neither did he swallow it. The flame bobbed. 'Please, Oscar,' I entreated.

His eyes held mine and for a moment I thought he wasn't going to listen, but then he swallowed the last drops. The tension drained out of him as the potion started to work instantly; no doubt his pounding headache had just dissipated. He flicked the lighter closed.

'Are you with us?' I asked cautiously.

He nodded but his eyes were guarded. 'What happened?'

I grimaced. 'It was my fault. We were attacked by a fire elemental. He sent a fireball towards us.'

'Towards your head,' Bastion corrected grimly. 'He wasn't mucking about, Amber. The heat from the fireball scorched my feathers. He was aiming to kill you. Even with your protective runes, you would have been a shish kebab.'

'Please, tell it like it is,' I said sarcastically. 'Don't sugar coat it for me.'

His lips twitched in amusement. 'You can take it.'

I could. I sat down heavily. 'I really thought that once my ORAL potion was out in the world, once it was patented, the attacks would stop.' Had I been naïve? 'I thought the Council was being foolish keeping you on, but I guess they know what they're doing.'

Bastion and Oscar exchanged a meaningful glance that I didn't understand. 'What?' I asked. 'What am I missing?'

My phone beeped with a text from Ethan. *I have one vial of brain-swelling potion left.* Well, wasn't he a donkey fornicator? I glared at the message then typed my response with hard jabs of my fingers. *No longer necessary. I have brewed my own batch. ADL.* I hoped the reproach for his delay in responding to me was clear.

I had intended to start on Ria's potion but I was exhausted after all the excitement. Adrenaline had left me feeling shocky and worn out, and I wanted to crawl into my bed with a good book. I regretted finishing *Dragon's Whored* the previous night.

'It's late,' I said. 'And it's been a long, emotional day.' Cindy's funeral seemed ages ago. I nodded at Oscar. 'You should get some rest. We'll walk you to your flat.'

Oscar crossed his arms. 'There's no need,' he groused. 'I'm not defenceless.' He took his lighter out of his pocket again and fired it up. He used the IR to grow the flickering light into a huge flame. 'See?'

I studied him. He didn't seem to remember using the same trick only moments earlier. Bastion shot me a grimace. Hopefully Oscar was just half-asleep rather than suffering some sort of brain damage. We'd have to assess him in the coming days, but the potion should have done its thing.

Now that Oscar was safe, the sudden appearance of flames in front of me made me react. I swallowed hard, struggling to get rid of the image of the deadly fireball roaring towards me. I heard my screams and the elemental's. He'd come to kill me but I'd killed him instead. I was numb now, but later...

What gave me the right to be judge, jury and executioner? Nothing. I was no better than Bastion: a killer. My mouth was dry and my heart was racing as I stared into the flames and loathed myself.

'Put it out!' Bastion barked sharply at Oscar. 'She's seen quite enough fire for one day.'

Oscar flinched. 'Sorry. I didn't think.'

'Evidently not,' Bastion growled.

'I'll see myself out,' Oscar said. I was still too shaken to argue with him.

'Amber,' Bastion's voice was soft. 'You're okay.' He was inches away. When had he gotten so close?

'Of course I am,' I responded but my voice lacked its usual certainty.

'Would you like a cup of tea?' he suggested.

I rustled up a small smile. 'Please.'

He busied himself in the kitchen whilst I returned to my lab to clean the cauldron. I desperately needed something else to focus on. I pulled on gloves and scrubbed the pewter until it shone, then cleaned my chopping boards, knives and worktops. It wouldn't do for the lab to be less than pristine.

I looked regretfully at the ingredients I'd bought earlier. Hopefully I would get to Ria's potion soon; she was safe in a magically-induced coma for now, but for how long? I contemplated pushing myself to try and brew it tonight, but swayed on my feet at the thought. If I attempted it now, I'd make mistakes and she couldn't afford for me to do that.

The potion Ria had ingested was black mordis, a poison that is invariably fatal. It had never been stopped – until now. Ria and her mousy familiar were still alive, albeit on borrowed time. I needed to create a potion to save them but it wasn't going to be tonight. I pushed disappointment in myself aside; I couldn't do everything.

I placed all the ingredients in stasis and put them under pre-runed bell jars, then pulled over my ladder so I could put some of the lesser-used ingredients on the top shelf. *A place for everything, and everything in its place.*

Once my lab was straight, I returned to the open-plan space. Bastion had set a mug of tea and a blueberry muffin on the table. Next to the muffin was a book. The man himself was conspicuously absent.

With no witnesses, I wasted no time examining the book. *The Curse of Amelie Jones.* The title seemed innocuous enough but I felt myself flush when I read the blurb. It seemed that Amelie was a witch who had been cursed with raging hormones. She needed a new and revolutionary potion to calm her explosive libido and the only one up to the task of making it was the reclusive Rick Cane, potioneer extraordinaire. Unfortunately, he was also the only man that she had despised because he'd stood her up on a date years ago. The book sold itself as a spicy, witchy, enemies-to-lovers romance. I normally avoided all things witchy since they were invariably wildly inaccurate, but I was in dire straits so I dived right in, sipping the calming tea as I read.

Bastion cleared his throat. 'Any good?'

I jumped as if I'd been electrocuted. 'Um...' My cheeks reddened. 'Great, thank you.' If I'd been alone I would have been reading the book one-handed and eating and drinking at the same time. I closed it and took a bite of the abandoned blueberry muffin; I'd long-since drunk the tea.

'Another brew before bed?' he offered.

'Yes, please.'

The escapism, tea and sugar had made me feel much better but weariness was dragging at my limbs. One last cuppa would be perfect.

Bastion passed me a hot brew in a mug which said *You're my lobster* and had a cartoon lobster blowing a kiss. I frowned; it wasn't one I remembered using before but I had so many mugs that wasn't surprising. Bastion must have had a good root around to find one that wasn't snarky or rude because those are a dime a dozen in my cupboards.

We finished our drinks in companionable silence before sliding into bed together. The silence stretched between us like a comforting blanket, warm and soft. I had never felt anything quite like it. Silences weren't warm, they were awkward and demanded to be filled. But not so with Bastion, with him I could just... be.

'Good night Amber,' he murmured eventually, ending this fragile moment between us.

'Good night.' I closed my eyes and hoped that the humour and romance of the book would chase away any impending nightmares.

They did not. I awoke and sat bolt upright, feeling flames on my skin and gasping for breath.

'Hey, you're okay. You're okay, Amber.' Bastion cautiously reached out and rubbed my back. I took a shuddering breath as I nodded and tried to stop the tears streaming down my face. This was *not* demonstrating my ability to utilise the British stiff upper lip. I palmed my cheeks, wiping away the tears while my chest still heaved. I hated that he was seeing me like this – that *anyone* would see me like this.

'I'm okay,' I repeated, my voice warbling. I didn't sound okay.

'Hey, it's okay to cry,' he murmured as he pulled me into the warmth of his body.

'No, it's not,' I said into his shoulder. 'Tears solve nothing.'

'They expunge the emotion from your body. It's healthy and necessary.' His voice was firm.

I snorted. 'Which is why you cry all the time.'

He stilled. 'I do, actually.' He lowered his voice so it was almost a whisper, and I knew he was about to tell me something intensely personal. 'When I'm particularly stressed or upset, I watch a movie to help me cry. There's a lot of toxic masculinity out there. The suicide rate is four times greater for men than women.'

Touching on suicide was a risky topic for us; after all, Bastion had coaxed the love of my life, Jake, to kill himself. Most of the time I managed to put that out of my mind and tried to focus on what I'd seen of Bastion since I'd got to know him: the way he'd cradled little toddler Frankie Marlow when he'd been found; the way he'd slept under my bed when I'd been scared of a bomb; the way he'd protected me even when his wings had singed to nothing... And now, the way he comforted me from my nightmares.

Bastion continued, 'It's okay for men to cry, too.'

I pushed up and looked at him, eyes wide. 'Of course it is! I didn't mean to imply that it wasn't.'

'No – but *you* don't think it's okay to cry.'

'It fine for anyone *else* to cry,' I explained hastily. 'But I try to be strong.'

'Why is crying weak?'

I had no answer and it was too late in the night to have my perspectives challenged, so I shifted the focus back to him. 'So what movies do you watch?'

He didn't point out the clumsiness of the change of topic. '*Schindler's List, The Green Mile, Steel Magnolias*, that sort of thing.'

'Have you ever watched *The Notebook*? Jinx loves it.'

I felt him nod. 'It's a good one.'

'I haven't seen it.' I didn't really have time for movies; I hadn't watched one in I didn't know how long.

'It might be difficult for you. There's dementia in it.'

Yeah, that would be hard. I hated the vile illness that stole a little more of my mum from me every day. 'It might be triggering,' I agreed, 'but I'd still like to watch it one day. It's one of Jinx's favourites.' Thinking about triggers pulled another stray thought forward. 'Have you heard of glimmers?' I asked curiously.

'Glimmer? Jinx's dagger?'

'No, not that. *A* glimmer, not *the* Glimmer. A glimmer is the opposite of a trigger. A glimmer is a moment in your day that sparks a sense of joy and wellbeing.' I shut my mouth before I could say that this moment, here with Bastion, was a glimmer. I had been terrified when I woke but now I felt calm, centred and safe. Something about him settled me.

We remained silent for a long while, lying next to each other, close but not touching. These still seconds between us are becoming something truly special to me. There is something so intimate about giving someone your silence. Listening to the steady thrum of your heartbeat and being present in the moment together, sharing the air with your breath. Finally I snuggled down. With my back to him, it was easier to say quietly, 'Thank you for sharing that with me.' It felt important, like he had peeled away a layer of vulnerability, just for me.

'You're welcome, Amber. Sleep well.' There was a pause. 'You're safe, I promise.'

I believed him. There seemed to be one or more people who wanted me dead but Bastion was determined to keep me alive. And my money was on him.

Chapter 6

'What do we know about the fire elemental?' Oscar asked as the three of us ate breakfast together.

'I sent his picture to Maxwell last night,' Bastion said. 'His face took some of the damage but it should be recognisable. Maxwell confirmed that it's not someone he immediately recognised, but he'll run it through the Pit database. He thinks it's a rogue.' The Pit is the fire elementals' governing body.

'That's why you went back to the body?' I asked. 'To ID him?'

'Yes – and to check whether he was dead. If he'd still been alive, we could have questioned him.'

'He took a potion bomb to the chest,' I pointed out flatly.

'Yeah. He *was* very dead.'

'Are there degrees of death?' I arched an eyebrow. Bastion shot me a look for my smart-assery. 'Have you come up against a fire elemental like this before?' I stopped myself from saying 'as a fellow assassin'.

'Rogues? They happen in every species, though admittedly there were no rogues under Benedict's rule.'

I snorted. Benedict had ruled the Pit before Roscoe took over and, thank the Goddess, he had caught a case of death. He had been a raving lunatic who revelled in death and torture. There had been no need for rogues under his rule; Benedict had been more than happy to give his stamp of approval on mayhem.

Oscar was quiet, buttering his crumpet and not saying a whole lot. 'Are you okay?' I asked him, suddenly worried. 'Is your head hurting?'

He smiled. 'I'm fine.' He said it like *I* always said it, which meant he wasn't fine at all but didn't want to talk about it. I respected his choice, but I thought about Bastion's quiet words in the dead of night. Who did Oscar have to talk to about his feelings, apart from Mum when she was having a good day? I added 'speak to Oscar about his feelings' to my mental to-do list. Some days there are so many things on that list it's a wonder my brain doesn't explode.

I checked my diary. The morning was fairly free; I was supposed to be teaching some coven children at 11am, but that was it. I chewed on my lip before I fired off a quick email from my phone asking Ethan or Venice to volunteer to cover the slot for me. I really needed a few clear hours.

'I'm going to do some potion making this morning,' I told Oscar. 'I'm not planning on going out. Why don't you visit Mum? I have Bastion with me.' Oscar looked uncertain. 'Go,' I repeated firmly.

'You won't leave the tower without me?'

'No,' I promised. 'I'm tower bound this morning.'

'Okay.' He seemed relieved. 'I'll go and see her.'

'Thanks. And tell her I love her. You know – if the moment is right.'

Oscar squeezed my hand. 'I will.' He went out, leaving me alone with Bastion.

Bastion leaned back in his chair, his dark eyes glittering as he looked at me. 'What are you going to do that you don't want Oscar to see?'

No one could fault his perception. 'Whatever it takes to get Ria back with us,' I said grimly. Including bloodletting, consulting with Grimmy, and anything else I could think of.

I was using my pewter cauldron again: pewter for healing. I was using the smallest one because this was a bespoke potion specifically keyed to Ria. Thanks to her mother's agreement, I had samples of both her hair and her blood.

My notebook was next to me and the potion base was bubbling away. It would be another hour before it would be ready for further ingredients. As I looked at my list, I couldn't help but feel that something was missing. I had so many ingredients and their interactions were highly complex, but I was definitely still missing something. The balance wasn't right.

I wasted another half hour flipping through the DeLea family potions book before admitting defeat. Frustrated, I turned the potion base down to simmer and stalked out of my lab, through my office and into my living-room area.

Bastion was doing one-armed push ups. My fit of pique fled.

He paused as he noted my entry. 'Everything okay?'

'Oh yes,' I responded, watching a bead of sweat drip down his arm. Oh heck! My voice sounded breathy. I coughed to hide it. 'I just need something from my bedroom.'

'The something in the safe?' His tone was curious but not pushy.

'Yes, that something. Don't let anyone in.'

'Roger that.'

I appreciated how he respected my boundaries. I went into the bedroom, shut the door and closed the curtains; only then did I key in the combination to the safe and open it. There were various notepads full of recipes for patented potions inside, as well as a host of usage license agreements. But the most important thing of all was Grimmy.

Grimmy is the sentient DeLea family grimoire who can recall every spell and every potion written into his pages. I'd already put the ORAL potion into his memory and he'd been pleased as punch at the addition.

There was a soft kraa behind my curtains and I peeked out to spy Fehu guarding the window that Bastion couldn't see. I gave him a little wave but then closed the curtains again to give me total privacy.

As I picked up the heavy tome and stroked his spine, Grimmy sprang to life. He rose up then hovered at eye level. Next he stretched, flicked his pages before coming to rest, then lay open with his middle pages exposed.

'Why Miss Amber, what a delight to see you again so soon! But in your bedroom again? You must not meet gentleman callers in such a way. You'll get a reputation.'

I resisted the urge to point out that he was a *book* and my virtue was about as safe as could be. 'Bastion is in the other room,' I explained.

'Why is that creature still here?' Grimmy sniffed disdainfully. 'He was to protect you when you were making the potion. The potion is made, ergo the danger should have passed.'

'Yeah – no. It's still very much here.' I told him about the fire elemental's attack.

'Outrageous!' His spluttering wrath was endearing. 'Who dares to target you still, Miss Amber?'

'If I were a betting girl, I'd bet everything on the black coven. I removed Ria from their grasp so they know I'm aware of their existence.'

'What are you going to do?'

'Hunt them down before they kill me,' I responded grimly.

'How?'

Wasn't that the million-dollar question? 'I'm not here to talk about that,' I said. 'I'm trying to make a potion to save Ria from the black mordis she swallowed. Things have become rather hectic lately.' I filled him in on all the recent events.

'Black mordis.' He drawled the potion's name. 'Miss Amber, you do pick the most delightful things to tangle with.'

'Go big or go home,' I responded drily.

'Indeed.' His pages fluttered as he thought. 'There is nothing in my pages that can help you directly,' he said finally. 'Not unless you're willing to stray into ... darker ... territory. The blood of an innocent, forcibly taken could—'

'No,' I interrupted firmly. 'Absolutely not. Move on. What else do you have?' I'd compromised my morals once before at Grimmy's behest; I'd saved Jake's life but the man who had come back to me hadn't been *my* Jake.

I'd riled him and his pages fluttered faster – then stilled abruptly. When he spoke, there was a hint of defeat in his tone. 'If you'd just consider—' He'd found nothing other than black magic to help me.

'No, I won't. The ends don't justify the means. I will never cause pain for my gain.'

'Not *your* gain, Miss Amber, but young Miss Ria Plath's. If you do not exercise flexibility with your morality, then I fear that Miss Ria will follow the same fate as Miss Sylvia of the same name.'

Sylvia Plath had been a poet and a feminist who had died tragically young in an era when mental health hadn't been properly understood and managed. Back then, the diagnosis of depression carried a stigma that thankfully it doesn't have today. My mum had been a big fan of hers and she'd even read some of her poetry to Grimmy, who insisted on remaining 'appropriately cultured'. He hadn't been thrilled when I had, tongue in cheek, tried to introduce him to rap music.

I glared at him. 'If you won't help me then I'll do it myself.'

'Do not be so hasty, Miss Amber.' His tone was thick with disapproval. 'I am more than the potions listed within me. Tell me about the one you're proposing to brew for Miss Ria.'

As requested, I ran through my ingredient list. 'What am I missing?' I demanded.

Grimmy thought for a moment. When he answered, his tone was grim. 'Death.'

'What? I'm trying to *save* her life, not end it!'

'You need something with the essence of death. All your ingredients are designed to bring life, but all potions must have balance – especially one such as yours. Ria's life is held in the balance and you must acknowledge that in the potion work.'

'Vampyr blood,' I murmured.

'That would be perfect – if they will give it to you,' Grimmy commented cynically.

'I'll ask nicely.'

'And if they say no?'

'I'll ask not so nicely,' I muttered darkly.

Chapter 7

I stroked Grimmy's spine in the opposite direction to send him to sleep, then opened the safe and settled him back inside. My childhood soft-toy was on the shelves, a black-and-white toy cat called Megan. It had been a gift from Aunt Abigay when I was struggling to come to terms with my lack of a familiar. As I gave Megan a little cuddle, I felt my heart rate slow.

I put her back in the safe, closed and locked it, then shut the cupboard door that hid it from the casual observer. I opened my bedroom curtains and waved at Fehu, who gave a little hop. I opened the window so he could hear me. 'All done,' I called out. He gave a kraa and flew off to do whatever it was that ravens do with their spare time.

'We need to see Wokeshire,' I told Bastion as I marched out of my room.

He'd used my interlude with Grimmy to have a quick shower and put on fresh clothes. The workout had obviously reinvigorated him. I can't get behind the idea of working out; I much prefer cake and a good book, which is why my body is soft. I prefer to think of it as roundly feminine.

'You promised Oscar we'd stay in the tower,' he pointed out.

I gnawed a fingernail. I *had* said that, and Oscar had a thing about lying, but still... Ria didn't have time for me to waste. 'I need something with the essence of death for my potion, so unless you have some vampyr blood in a blood bag somewhere I don't know about...'

'No – but what about a clipping from one of my talons? You couldn't get much more deadly than that.'

I blinked. To my knowledge, no griffin had ever volunteered any piece of themselves for potion work – and no one had been foolish enough to try and take something forcibly. A claw, with its hardened state, would take longer to work into the potion but it would also stabilise it more. It was perfect, even better than vampyr blood. 'That would absolutely work,' I breathed. 'Will you give it to me?'

'Of course.' His eyes shone gold as he shifted his right hand into a talon.

'Hang on.' I bustled into my bathroom and pulled out a manicure set complete with clippers.

Bastion looked at the pink set with amusement. 'They're not going to cut through my claw.'

'You'd be surprised. Sit down and hand me your ... claw.'

He sat and lifted the deadly thing towards me. Because I'd been spending more time with him, the talon didn't fill me with jabbering terror the way it once might have done. I held up the nail clippers but, sure enough, there was no way in hell they would cut through his claw. It was way too thick.

He kindly didn't say 'I told you so', then lifted up a trouser leg to expose a deadly-looking blade resting in an ankle holster. He pulled it out.

'Why do you carry a knife?' I asked. 'You have claws.'

'I can't throw my talons.' He eyed the large knife and eyeballed the distance between us. 'Move back a little.' He brought the blade down forcefully, making me squeak a little, then handed me a sharp shard of nail about an inch long. 'Is that enough?'

I nodded. 'I think so.'

His cut had left a sharp jagged edge on his finger, which looked unseemly. I pulled out the nail file and rounded it off so at least it didn't look silly. Bastion let me do it with an odd expression on his face, but when he caught me looking at him he pasted on a smirk. 'I'm out of here if you pull out a bottle of nail varnish,' he joked.

'What about your battle with toxic masculinity?'

'It doesn't extend to nail varnish,' he said drily. 'It's hard to inspire fear with sparkly nails.'

A smile tugged at my lips. 'I reckon you could do it.'

'Challenge not accepted.'

I snickered. Picking up the chunk of claw, I sobered abruptly. 'Thank you.' A griffin giving a piece of himself was a big deal and I didn't want him to think I was taking it lightly.

'No problem.' He gave me a lazy half smile that made my tummy flutter; obviously I must be hungry.

I had no time to eat. I made my way back to the lab with my missing ingredient in tow. It was time to finish this potion.

Chapter 8

I had just finished cooling and decanting the potion when my phone rang. I frowned when I saw that it was Hilary Mitchell calling me. She was an old, ornery witch who had a barren field of effs. She had no effs left to give. She was often rude and abrasive and, as such, I didn't have much time for her. However, she was also on the coven Council, a position that demanded my respect. I had never had a Council member call me directly before; they preferred to let their PAs do their scut work.

My gut tightened with anxiety and I hastily swiped to answer. 'Amber DeLea.'

'Amber, you need to come to Edinburgh – now.' Her voice was forceful and harsh. Before I could ask why I was being summoned, she continued. 'Abigay is dying.'

The world fell away and I sat down heavily. 'What?' My voice was a whisper. Abigay couldn't be dying. She was eighty but I'd seen her only a matter of days ago and she'd been as strong as a centaur on steroids.

'She's been cursed. I can't counter it, nor can she. You need to come. To The Witchery. Now.'

'Put her in stasis, and then—'

'Don't teach me to suck eggs, child! *Isa* has failed on her. The runes slide off. I don't need you to bring sand to the beach. Abigay has been runed with *angrepet*.'

A black rune. Goddess wept. Abigay was being killed by a black witch, someone she had known and trusted enough to let them get close enough for them to rune her. 'By whom?'

'Don't you think I've asked all of these questions? You're wasting time and Abigay has very little left. She's asking for you. I pray you'll make it in time.' Hilary's tone made it clear that she thought I had no chance of doing so. With that, she hung up.

Still in shock, I grabbed a decanted vial of Ria's potion and moved towards my lounge. As I paused at the threshold, trying to order my jumbled thoughts, I heard Oscar and Bastion talking. Good: that meant Oscar was back from visiting Mum. I opened my mouth to speak but froze as I overheard their conversation.

'You need to tell her the truth,' Oscar said harshly to Bastion.

'What truth?' Bastion's response was cool.

'You know exactly what I'm talking about. It's keeping you apart.'

There was a pause. 'That's the place we need to be.'

'Bullshit. For someone who is knocking on two hundred years old, you're not very wise. I won't stand by and let you hurt her. She should have been my daughter – hell, she *is* my daughter. If you don't wise up and tell her then I will.' Oscar's tone was forceful.

There was a low growl. 'I don't respond well to threats.'

'I'll remember that next time I'm threatening you. Bastion, pull your head out of your ass. Trust her enough to be truthful.'

'I'm not the only one with secrets, Oscar. People made of paper shouldn't throw fireballs.'

I felt like the rug had been pulled out from under me. Both men were hiding something from me, something important. I'd trusted Oscar since I was a child, and to know he was keeping secrets from me was devastating. And Bastion? I'd reluctantly started to trust him – how could I not with all we'd been through together? But now

I cursed myself. Trust was for fools, and damn me for being one of them.

I didn't have time for this. Screw them. Whatever their secrets were, they could keep them. Abigay was dying, Ria was dying – I had no time to waste.

I strode into the room and they both looked up, faces blank. Heck, they'd both looked at me like that before. How many times had they whispered their secrets behind my back? Hurt sliced through me as sharp as the blade that the dryad had stabbed me with – and this hurt more.

I swallowed. 'Abigay is dying. She's been cursed. We need to go to Edinburgh immediately, but I have this vial and it needs to be taken to Ria also immediately. I can't give it to another witch – I don't trust anyone.' How true that sentence was now.

The potion had Ria's hair and blood in it, a combination that meant it was keyed to her personally. That vastly increased its efficacy but shortened its shelf life; even with an *isa*, she needed to consume it within a day. If I gave it to Jeb or Ethan or Venice and one of them turned out to be the black witch, I'd be handing them Ria on a plate and her death would be a certainty.

The men exchanged rueful glances that I didn't understand or care about at that moment. 'If I take the time to save Ria, I won't see Abigay before she dies.' My voice faltered on the last word as a sob broke through.

'I'll take it to her,' Oscar offered. 'You go to Edinburgh, to Abigay.' He turned to Bastion. 'And you guard her with your life.' He said the last words through gritted teeth. He hated leaving me in someone else's care.

I nodded briskly like my heart wasn't dying in my chest. 'Yes. That's the only solution. Thank you.' I thrust the vial at Oscar. 'You'll have to get it tested. Melva will fit you in. You know where Ria and Meredith are. Make sure you're not followed. Please stay with Ria and report back on her recovery.'

Or lack thereof. I truly believed that the potion would work, but the seer priestess could confirm that it wouldn't do any harm to Ria and whether it would be efficacious. However, the exact degree to which it would help could only be determined by taking it.

Oscar took the vial. Rather than swiftly heading for the door, he came close and gave me an uncharacteristic fierce hug. 'I love you,' he said with bundle of emotion in his voice. It was so tangled that I couldn't un-weave it, but I couldn't recall him ever saying those words to me.

My mouth dropped open before my brain engaged, then I frowned instead. 'Maybe you still have a head injury.'

He barked a sudden laugh. 'I'm fine.' He kissed me on the forehead. 'Go, be with Abigay. I'll be in touch.' He walked out.

Bastion stared at me. 'Your reaction to being told that someone loves you is to query whether or not he has a brain injury?'

I folded my arms. 'He's never said it before.'

'That doesn't mean he hasn't felt it.'

'No, but the timing of the confession is weird.'

'Not really. He's leaving your side for the first time in a decade or so. He's worried.'

'We're apart often enough,' I argued.

'Not when you're in danger,' Bastion pointed out. 'Not like this. It's hard for him to leave you with me.'

'Why?' I demanded. Because of their secrets?

'Because he knows I don't feel the same way towards you as he does.'

That hurt a little more than it should have done; obviously Bastion didn't *love* me – we were just friends. Or we had been; now I wasn't sure what we were.

I didn't have time for any of this BS. This was why friends and feelings were a waste of life. 'None of this is important,' I snarled. 'We need to get to Edinburgh!'

'We do,' he agreed. 'I can get us a helicopter but it will take time to arrive.'

'What other option is there?' In despair, I blew out a harsh breath.

'Griffin Air.'

Chapter 9

I'd ridden on Shirdal plenty of times, but it felt completely different to throw myself astride Bastion and I didn't want to examine why. I just needed to get to Edinburgh as quickly as possible.

Bastion was still in human form. He handed me some sort of leather harness that he had stowed in his go-bag. Attached to it were two stirrups. 'We're in a hurry,' he said, 'so I'll be going as fast as I can. You won't be able to stay on without help. When I shift, I'll step into the harness. You'll need to secure it around my neck and body using these buckles. Here, and here.' He pointed to them and I nodded.

We were standing on the coven roof. The April day was so warm that I'd only been wearing a blouse, but Bastion had forced me to don extra layers. The wind would be significantly cooler up high, and we'd be airborne for a while.

Bastion passed me some goggles, which made me grimace, and I took them reluctantly. I'd packed my potions and brushes into a black backpack. Impatience was chafing at me, even though it had only taken a handful of minutes for us to prepare since Oscar's departure.

Bastion laid the harness on the floor with practiced ease and then he shifted. This time his leonine form did not fill me with fear. I stepped forward and pulled the harness up his legs before he could instruct me, buckled the strap at his neck first then the one around his body. After I'd carefully untangled the stirrups, I lay them to either side of his huge white wings. There wasn't a charred feather amongst them; he was all healed up after the fireball's destruction.

That reminder of the attack made me falter. Did the whispered conversation between Oscar and Bastion undo all the good that Bastion had done? He was keeping a secret from me; I was keeping Grimmy from him. We all had secrets.

I shook my head to clear it. Not now. None of this mattered now. I clipped the chest strap onto my backpack and secured the goggles over my eyes. I tied back my hair, then slung my leg over his back and slipped my feet into the stirrups. Leaning down low on his back, I reached forward for the raised loop of leather and gripped it tightly.

When I'd thought about getting my leg over Bastion, this hadn't been what I'd envisaged. Not that I'd envisaged anything. 'Ready,' I shouted into the wind. 'Go!'

'Hold on,' he instructed gruffly.

Obviously. 'I'm holding already. Go!' I repeated urgently.

I had expected him to flap his wings to lift off but he wanted to gain speed as quickly as possible. His strong lion's body broke into a run and *then,* when we were already running at speed, his wings snapped out. They started flapping moments before he leapt off the edge of the building and I stifled the scream that wanted to erupt. Even so, a mouse-like squeak escaped me.

His wingspan was huge and the powerful downdraft he created was astonishing. In moments we were up, up and away. I clung on with all of my might and thought fondly of the firm ground already thousands of metres below me. How high were we going? Above the Common realm's sight, I realised. We were high enough for the Verdict – the magic that hides the Other realm – to whisper into the Common realmers' minds that they were seeing a bird or a plane rather than a woman astride a magical griffin.

I clung on and prayed that we would reach Abigay in time.

Edinburgh looked different from above, but the castle was an easy landmark. Bastion made a beeline for it because The Witchery was just around the corner. My legs were uncomfortable from being splayed open for so long; let's face it, it was the most action they'd had in years. I would ache tomorrow, and not in a fun way. It was difficult to tell how long the journey had taken, an hour maybe two, but quicker than we could have got here by helicopter. Bastion was *fast*.

We came in to land by the castle. As we touched down, Bastion shifted and tilted me from his back. He caught me before I staggered and fell. He unhooked the harness and bundled it up before stuffing it into his own backpack which I hadn't noticed before the shift. I tore off my goggles and handed them to him and they disappeared into the backpack too.

There were tourists milling around. 'Wow!' someone shouted. 'Did you see that? BASE jumpers!'

'Where's your parachute?' another man asked in confusion.

Bastion grinned. 'We handed it to someone in the crowd to get rid of. BASE jumping into the castle is illegal. You didn't see a thing.' He tossed them a wink.

'Cool!'

We merged with the crowd and headed hastily towards The Witchery, where I prayed Abigay was still waiting for us.

Chapter 10

The Witchery was open for lunch and already doing a roaring trade. I ignored it all – Rosemary's sympathetic expression and the hush of the subdued acolytes. I took the stairs two at a time, hoping that I wasn't too late.

I burst into Abigay's room and nearly sobbed when she turned her head towards me. I saw the spidery network of black mordis in the veins around her bright eyes. Despite that, her lips were still painted her signature bright pink. Even when she was dying, Abigay wanted to look her finest.

Hilary was holding her hand. She looked up, her eyes red rimmed and haunted by grief. 'You took your time,' she snapped.

'I can't teleport!' I snarled.

'Evidently not,' she shot back.

'I envy those that haven't met you,' I huffed under my breath.

Not quietly enough, apparently. 'Back at you. I wish we were better strangers!'

'Ladies,' Abigay snorted. 'That's quite enough. Tempers are high because I'm dying but if anyone gets to throw a hissy fit, it will be me.' Her familiar, Elias, a tortoiseshell cat, let out an anguished mrrow. He was nestled into her side and she was stroking his fur. It was the end for both of them but Elias's sole concern was for her.

Remorse bit through me. 'I'm sorry, Abigay.' I brushed my hair out of my eyes and pulled a chair closer to her bedside. 'What can we do?' I reached out and gave Elias a quick stroke hello. He raised his head as I stroked and batted his head into my hand. My heart aching, I gave him a few more scritches.

'You two can work together to find out who killed me,' Abigay said grimly. 'I want my killer or killers found and punished. You promise me that.'

'Of course.' Hilary and I spoke in unison.

Abigay nodded with satisfaction. 'By chance, Hilary found *angrepet* painted on the small of my back. She saw a flash of it when I leaned over and my top rose up a little. She has tried to counter it, or to cancel it, but with no luck. Someone must have breached my wards whilst I was sleeping. Hilary and I drank too much last night. It was an unfortunate mistake.'

'But it was a fun one.' Hilary smiled. 'You sang so beautifully.'

'A shame I didn't make it to the ceilidh. I would have if I'd known it would be my last.' The old friends exchanged a fond look.

'I had fun enough for you,' Hilary promised.

Abigay smiled before turning back to the matter of deathly runes. 'We've tried but we've been unable to remove the black rune, and it appears to have been painted on in black mordis. It's soaked in completely now.'

I closed my eyes, shaking with despair. I wanted to wail and gnash my teeth. 'I brewed an antidote to black mordis this morning.' It had been keyed to Ria, but maybe if I'd known I could have separated some of it before I'd added her blood and hair. Rune ruin! What a mess.

'There is no antidote,' Hilary argued.

'There is never anything until someone invents it. If you'd told me on the phone what you'd suspected...' Grief made me lash out and anger darkened my tone. I wouldn't have had time to brew it all over again in time to save

Abigay, but grief needs a culprit. I didn't have a black witch handy so Hilary would have to do.

'Shoulda, woulda, coulda.' Abigay waved it away. 'I consulted with the Goddess. It is my time. There is nothing to be done.'

'I don't believe in prophecy,' I snarled.

'Prophecy or fate – whatever you call it, child, it believes in you.'

'I can save you,' I said stubbornly. I hauled Grimmy half out of my backpack and Hilary's eyes widened at the sight of the heavy tome.

'Amber ... no.' Abigay reached out and pressed my hand, pushing Grimmy back into the confines of the bag.

'There's a rune, a black one—' The one I'd used to save Jake. Where were my morals now, with Abigay's life on the line? And what did that make me that I hadn't straddled that line for Ria?

'No!' Abigay snarled in a dark voice I'd rarely heard.

The vehemence of her cry took me aback. 'Abigay... I can't lose you.' Tears burned my eyes.

'The black runes do not simply give life – they take something in order to work, Amber. Always.'

I nodded. I knew that better than most. I scrubbed at my tears in frustration. She was right. Jake had lived but he had not *lived*.

'Besides, you will not lose me, princess.' Abigay's voice softened. 'I am with you now and always. The ones we love live on in our heart. You will hear my voice and remember my smile. I may be gone but I will not be forgotten.'

She gasped and her mouth twisted as a wave of pain rocked her. 'There are things you must know. You must speak to Oscar about your father. Your mother was … selective with the truth.' She met my eyes. 'It's time to put your mother's oath skills to the test,' she said grimly. She visibly braced herself. 'Your father was a black witch, Amber.'

I felt like my whole foundation was being pulled from under me. How could my mum have lied to me about *this*?

'Your mother was distraught when she found out what he'd been practising. He didn't leave you – your mum forced him out. She didn't want him to influence you, to raise you in the black arts, so she kicked him to the kerb. She kept a safety deposit box – I don't know where – but in it you'll find evidence of his dark practices. I have no doubt that he's involved in the black coven and you need to destroy it.' As she spoke each word, shadows seemed to thicken until a black energy around her pulsed with malevolence.

The black shadows were a harbinger of an oath death. To break an oath is almost unthinkable because death by broken oath is agonising and inevitable. There is no healing, no rune, no potion that can save you from a broken oath.

I closed my eyes in despair. There would be no saving her from this. As if black mordis hadn't been enough... I shoved aside the pity party; she was still alive *now*. By telling me about my father's black practices, she had broken the oath. Now I had only a few moments left with her on this earth, I wanted to talk about happy memories and make her smile. But time was so damned short and I needed information.

Hating myself, I asked, 'You know about the black coven? What can you tell me about them?'

'I have long suspected their existence. Over the years, as I moved up and down the country hunting black witches, I found evidence of collusion though never enough to bring before the Council. When the first witch mentioned the black coven, I hoped that it was bullshit, but over the years it has come up time and time again. I hunted the members but it was like playing whack-a-mole – every time I got one, another popped up in their place. They are organised and united and it needed more than one old woman to bring the black coven to its knees. Lately I have had the feeling that something big is coming. They're making a play for power. I think my death is evidence of that.'

The black energy surged around her; now most of her body was covered in shadows and only her chest, shoulders, neck and face were visible. She coughed and hacked up some blood. As Hilary leant over and wiped Abigay's face with a handkerchief, I saw it was already covered in bloodstains.

When the coughing fit subsided, Abigay spoke again. 'I was poking my nose into the bees' nest, but I didn't expect them to sting me so quickly or effectively. I was sloppy, careless.' She fixed Bastion with her piercing stare. 'You must keep Amber safe. Do *not* leave her side. Not for anything. Do you hear me, griffin?'

Bastion nodded, his eyes grim. 'My life before hers,' he vowed.

Abigay smiled in satisfaction before gasping again. Another coughing fit wracked her and more blood spewed from her mouth. 'We don't have much time,' she grimaced. 'The oath death is coming far faster than I thought it would. Amber, I was loud in my hunt for the black witches these last few weeks, sick to death of the cloak-and-dagger routine. But their response was sudden and vicious. You must be careful,' She squeezed my hand and looked me in the eyes. 'It is your destiny to weed out these witches. There was a prophecy. Seek it.'

She saw the stubborn set of my jaw. 'Seek it!' she insisted. 'You must. You cannot deny your fate.' She coughed again. When she regained her breath, she met my eyes with a piercing stare. 'Your father…'

I glared. She wanted to talk about that waste of space *now*? 'He's not important.'

She hacked up a glob of blood. 'He is!' she insisted. 'You must listen, even against your instincts … because they are not your own.'

'What do you mean?' I frowned. I tried to think about my father but it felt as if my thoughts were sliding away from me. I gnawed my lip as realisation dawned: someone had spelled me.

'Abigay… I don't even remember his name…' And surely that should have been a red flag. Why hadn't I been more curious about him or tried to reach out to him as I'd grown older? I'd never had the slightest inclination to see him after he'd abandoned us. But I was six when he left and I should still remember his name.

'Luna had your mind cleared,' Abigay confessed. 'She didn't want you finding him later in life, and she had him blackmailed so he didn't dare approach you.' Her words were slow and laboured and her eyes were fluttering, as if it were taking everything she had to prise them open against a heavy weight.

I was in a maelstrom of emotion. Abigay was dying before my eyes, and my own mother had *wiped my mind*. And not just of a traumatic experience – oh no, Mum had wiped out my father's very *name*. I could still picture him but even that was the faintest recollection. I thought he'd been blond, with a roguish smile and my own green eyes.

'My heart is slowing,' Abigay gasped. She met Bastion's eyes. 'The oath death may kill me or the black mordis, but what I know is that if I die at the hands of the black witches' rune, they will use my life force to boost their powers. I have no wish for my death to give them any gain. Please, Bastion, kill me before they do or before the broken oath takes me. I do not want to die officially foresworn.'

Bastion hesitated, looking at me not for permission but with concern. I swallowed hard but I nodded to give him the licence he wasn't requesting. I understood what Abigay meant, what she was feeling. I wouldn't want my murderers to benefit from my death either, nor would I want an oath breaker's rune in the book of names.

I leaned forward and kissed her forehead. 'I love you, Aunt Abigay.' My voice choked. 'You were the best auntie a girl could ask for. I'm so grateful I had you in my life.'

Abigay smiled. 'As am I, princess, as am I. On a good day, tell your mum I loved her too.'

I nodded through tears and a broken heart.

Bastion moved forward, transforming his right hand to his talons. He lifted the blanket and sliced efficiently through Abigay's femoral artery. She gasped at the sharp cut but then sank back on the bed. 'That's not so bad. Thank you, Bastion.'

He nodded once then stepped back into the shadows to allow Hilary and me to be there for her last moments. Hilary leaned over and pressed a kiss onto her best friend's forehead. 'I'm sorry, my dear,' she murmured. 'I'll never forget you.'

The pulsing black shadows had moved up to Abigay's neck now and only her face was clear. I was scared the broken oath would take her instead of Bastion.

'I love you, Aunt Abigay,' I repeated, desperate for her to know the truth. I hadn't said it often enough, and now it was too late I wanted to cram in a lifetime of I love yous.

But it wasn't enough. The words spilled out of me and hot tears were trying to fall. I blinked them away as best I could but it was a losing battle. I pawed at my cheeks. I didn't want the last thing she saw to be me sobbing.

Abigay smiled, those bright pink lips turning up in a dazzling beam. 'And I love you, princess.' She tugged at the necklace around her neck. 'Here, take this – I want you to have it. Daughter of my heart, I'm so proud of you. I always have been. You'll do great things, Amber.' Her grin widened. 'Though next time, name your life-changing potion a little more carefully...'

She surprised a snort out of me, half laugh and half sob. I leaned forward and kissed her forehead again. She struggled upright a little so I could unfasten the necklace from her neck. The small charm that hung from it was still warm from her.

Bastion stepped forward and secured it around my neck. Abigay looked pleased at that. 'You mustn't close your heart to love,' she murmured. I wasn't sure who she was talking to, or if it was just a general observation.

She coughed and spluttered; when she stopped, she was gasping and wheezing. She let out a whimper of pain and it slayed me. The black energy was around her mouth making it look like she was breathing in thick black foulness.

Tears stung my eyes. 'Please, Bastion,' I whispered. 'End it ... before she is taken.'

Bastion stepped forward and looked at Abigay with glowing golden eyes. 'Relax,' he coaxed. 'Go.'

Abigay looked at me. Her eyes now glowed golden too, seized by Bastion's magic. She smiled tenderly. Her chest heaved one last time and then it didn't rise again. As suddenly as it had appeared, the malevolent blackness retreated, disappearing like a shadow in the face of the sun. It was as if it had never existed.

Aunt Abigay's body was still; the spark that had animated her had gone. What lay before me wasn't my Aunt Abigay but an empty corpse.

My heart hurt and tears fell down my face unbidden and unchecked.

Aunt Abigay was gone.

Chapter 11

Hilary and I were both crying. I scarcely noticed the tears that streamed down my face. Abigay had half-raised me. She had sneaked me cookies when my mother wasn't looking. She had taught me to tell the time and given me my first watch. And when it had become apparent that I wasn't going to have my own familiar, she'd bought me a toy cat to snuggle with at night.

Elias's little body had stilled, too. I gave him a stroke of farewell and pressed a kiss to his delicate head. Goddess, but it hurt. Abigay had lived a full life and she was an old woman, but I wasn't ready to say goodbye to her, not by a long shot. She should have lived to a hundred, at least. She had such a joie de vivre; it was wrong that she had been torn from us so soon.

Grief and fury vied for my attention. I pushed the grief away and pulled the rage close. 'I'm going to find them and

I'm going to put an end to them – one way or another,' I vowed in a bitter whisper.

Hilary looked up and met my eyes; hers were full of sharp, spikey grief. 'Her diary. She's always so organised – *was* so organised. She'll have kept notes about who she'd been talking to.'

'Who she may have freaked out,' I noted.

Hilary nodded. 'It's in the nightstand.'

Even though it felt macabre to root through Abigay's things whilst her body still lay before us, I opened the drawer of the bedside table. There was a small potion vial, which I pocketed, but no diary.

'There's no diary here,' I said. I didn't mention the vial. Hilary and I didn't always see eye to eye and she might want it for herself, or she might want to give it back to the potion store.

Hilary swore darkly then walked over to Abigay's dresser and started looking through it. The more she looked, the more agitated she became. Finally, after she'd torn through all of the cupboards and wardrobes, she shook her head. 'It's gone. They must have taken it.'

My jaw clenched and a swear word tried to bubble up. I did some deep breathing to push it down. I'd never known Abigay to keep a diary – she'd had a mind like a steel trap

– but maybe old age had changed her habits. Even in my forties, I found myself walking into my lab and standing there wondering what had brought me there. In her eighties, maybe she'd finally succumbed to a poor memory and started taking notes. If she had, and they had been taken, then her killer's name was probably included in them.

I turned to Hilary. 'Can you formally notify Rosemary for me? And make arrangements for her body and Elias's? I'd like a moment alone with them.'

Hilary nodded in understanding. 'Of course.' She made her way out of the door on unsteady feet.

I waited until she'd left before saying to Bastion, 'Help me roll her over. I want to look at the runes on her back.' I refused to call the body by Abigay's name; it wasn't Abigay, not now. I had to think like that or I wouldn't be able to look at the body clinically.

Bastion's mouth tightened but he said nothing as he gently turned her over. Feeling like an invader, I lifted up her pyjama top.

Angrepet was scrawled on her back in careful strokes. I studied the rune style; there were no whorls or embellishments like my mother favoured, instead it was strict and utilitarian. Next to it was Hilary's *ezro* and *isa*. Two runes, basic but flawless, yet they'd failed. Truthfully, the issue may not even have been the *angrepet* but the black mordis it had been painted with. Ria had swallowed it but that had been overkill; black mordis is a deadly, fast-acting, contact poison and it doesn't need to be imbibed to work.

I grabbed my backpack, pulled out a potion and a paintbrush and quickly painted on *perthro* – the revelation rune – over the top of the *angrepet*. A magical signature floated before my eyes and I stared at it, committing it to memory. A witch's magical signature is an intensely personal thing; asking to see it is like demanding to know what fantasies get your rocks off and it just isn't done. But once I found a suspect, I'd tear their signature from them anyway. I was going to emulate Hilary and give precisely zero fucks. I would stop at nothing to get Abigay's killer where they belonged – six feet under.

I wiped off the *perthro* with a baby wipe. The *angrepet* didn't change or disappear under the wipe; it was dark and stained onto her back like a tattoo. Once the *angrepet* was no longer active, it would only be a matter of minutes before the magical signature faded to nothing. Now at least I had a lead. 'Lay her back down,' I instructed Bastion.

He did so. 'Don't you trust Hilary?' he asked.

'I don't trust anyone.' The words exploded out of me, brittle and bitter and harsh. With my heart aching, it felt woefully true. Another day, I'd confront him about his exchange with Oscar but now it had just left me feeling lost and hurt.

I touched my hand to The Witchery's walls and drew forth my magic. Abigay's wards lit up like a Christmas tree but already they were starting to fade. She was gone and her magic was gone with it. I hastily examined the ward runes before they disappeared completely and frowned.

'What's the matter?' Bastion asked.

'The wards haven't been breached. There's not a single *ezro* painted anywhere. They were operating at full force.'

'The Crone thought that they'd been interfered with,' Bastion mused with a frown.

'Yes, but they hadn't been. Whoever slipped into the room and painted the rune on her was someone she trusted enough to add into her wards.'

'Or she allowed them entrance. Or – just to play devil's advocate – the rune was painted on her somewhere else.'

'That's possible,' I conceded. 'Though unlikely. Black mordis is fast acting. The chances of her surviving it through the night and into the day if it was painted on her *before* she went to bed?' I shook my head. Slim to non-existent.

I stared at Abigay's body, but she had gone. She didn't even *look* like Abigay anymore; that thing that had animated her – be it a soul or whatever else you want to call it – had gone. I couldn't bear to see her looking like a shell of herself. It cut to see her body so still and motionless.

I took a spare white sheet from the cupboard – I'd seen it when Hilary was rifling through Abigay's belongings – shook it out and gently laid it over her and Elias. In seconds the blood from Bastion's wound had soaked into the pristine sheet and turned it red. It looked sinister and forbidding. I sat next to her bed for a long moment.

Hilary finally walked back in. Her mouth tightened as she took in the covered body then she gave a soft sigh.

I stood. 'I'll notify the Council of her passing. Will you stay with her? I hate the thought of her being alone.'

Hilary's eyes softened. 'Of course. I'll contact the undertakers. We'll build a pyre for her tonight.'

Fire is cleansing; it would remove the last traces of black magic from her. I nodded, my throat too scratchy and raw for me to speak. A lot of Abigay's family were still in the Caribbean and witches' funerals are always carried out promptly, a leftover from darker times. The fire ensures that the body is not reanimated by a stray necromancer. Today that seemed like a very valid fear.

It felt like the black witches were *everywhere.* I prayed that Ria had exaggerated the truth and that Abigay was wrong but, no matter how many black witches there were, I'd make it my life's work to take them down.

Every single one.

Chapter 12

The underground city was quiet. It felt hushed, and rightly so, though there was no way that its residents could already know of Abigay's passing.

The death of the Crone would plunge us into formal mourning and start the lengthy selection process for her replacement. Hilary stood a good chance of being the next one to be pushed into power because she was already on the Council, already respected. Traditionally the Crone was someone in their sixties or over and who'd never had children of their own; the coven became their children. Hilary was married, but it was acceptable to have a husband.

I thought about who else was in the running: Beatrice Wraithborne, certainly, and there were plenty of other candidates. It wasn't unusual for a witch to choose power over starting a family. Beatrice was on the Council too, and had butted heads with Abigay on numerous occasions, often voting against Abigay's guidance.

There would also be witches who were not on the Council, like Abigay. She had come to the Crone role without ever serving on it. Eleanora Moonspell, perhaps? She was a fixture at the underground markets and was widely respected.

I was unsure whether I was listing them as potential Crones or potential suspects. People killed for ambition, didn't they? Had one of them sought to clear a path to the Crone's coveted position?

Bastion walked behind me as we wound our way to the Council. This time when Rosemary told him to wait, he simply walked past her and ignored her indignant spluttering that the hidden city was just for witches. She was wrong, of course; Benji lived there, too. Benji is a golem, constructed of nothing more than clay and magic.

As we approached the hall of the coven Council, he stood there absolutely still like a powered-down sentinel. His magic flicked out and sizzled as it touched me. Like a motion detector, it sounded an alarm at our approach and woke him.

Benjamin Cohen stands a solid 6ft 5in tall. His rough-hewn body was dressed in a black T-shirt and black suit trousers, but his huge feet were enclosed in special boots that somewhat ruined the ensemble. His smile as he saw me was beatific, and I found myself smiling back a little despite the circumstances.

'Am!' he greeted me. He'd no doubt cut off the 'Bam' when he saw Bastion loitering behind me.

'Benji,' I responded warmly. 'It's good to see you.' I was surprised by how true that was. I needed a friend, today more than ever.

'Are you okay, Am?' Benji studied me with concern. 'Your eyes and nose are red. This indicates tears. Have you been crying?'

Wonderful. It's always good to know you look like crap. I nodded. 'The Crone is dead.'

His eyes, the colour of earth, rolled at me with too much empathy. How could anyone say he was rock and clay and nothing else? He held open his arms and I stepped into them, then he wrapped his cold, solid arms around me. 'Friends comfort each other when they're sad, Am Bam,' he whispered into my ear. 'I'm so sorry.'

I nodded against his shoulder and suddenly the tears were back, gushing out of me in a deluge that I couldn't have stopped if I'd tried. Grief, hot and raw, swamped me and I sobbed whilst I clung to Benji for dear life.

I couldn't tell you how long I stayed in his embrace but when I eventually pushed back I felt a little better. Maybe Bastion was right about this crying thing.

Benji's warm eyes studied me with concern and touched a finger to my cheek. 'Okay, friend?'

'I'm okay, Benji. Thank you.' I pressed a kiss to his cheek and stepped back.

He raised his thick fingers to his cheek, to the place where I had kissed him. 'I have never had a kiss before. It was very nice. I see why they are enjoyed.'

'There are different types of kisses,' Bastion said. 'That was a friendly one – one between friends.'

Was it my imagination or was there a slight edge to Bastion's voice? If I hadn't known better, I'd have said he was jealous but that would have been absurd.

The tears had left a dull ache in my head, though my heart felt a little lighter and I was in charge of my faculties again. I brushed the dampness from my face; there was nothing I could do about the redness of my eyes and nose, nor did I want to. I wore my grief like a badge. Let the world know how much I had loved Aunt Abigay.

I took a steadying breath. 'I need to see the Council, Benji. Is it convened?'

'It will be ready to see you in a moment,' he confirmed. 'I summoned them when I saw you.'

'Thank you.'

'How did she die?' His voice was openly curious like a child's.

'She was poisoned.'

His eyes widened. 'Someone murdered her?' He spoke the word 'murdered' in a disbelieving whisper.

I nodded.

'Who would do such a thing? She was such a kind soul.'

'A black witch,' I said, deliberately speaking in the singular. I didn't need the black coven to be aware that I knew there was a whole coven full of festering, rotting witches.

Benji looked grim. 'You'll find the killer.'

I nodded briskly. 'I will.'

His eyes flashed white for a moment. 'The Council awaits you, Amber DeLea.' Then they flashed back to his own warm brown. 'And you are ready for them.'

I smiled at his reassurance, though I didn't need it. *I* was ready for *them*, and for all that was coming.

Chapter 13

The coven Council chamber was deliberately dimly lit. The underground city had electricity and running water so it could have been lit up like the fourth of July, but they kept it dark, creating an ominous feel. I guess they just liked to be welcoming.

The room was sparsely furnished, with a raised dais and a host of ornately carved wooden chairs set out in a semi-circle. A solitary chair sat in the centre of the room; this one was very plain and sat on a blood-red rug. I had no doubt that the rug hid a pentagram with activated truth runes – I'd learnt my chair trick from the best. I felt the urge to spill my secrets as soon as I walked forward, but I pulled them closer and maintained my harsh silence.

I sat on the rickety chair and Bastion took up position by the door. Thirteen chairs surrounded me in a semi-circle. The middle chair, larger and grander than the rest, was empty. That was the chair I coveted most; not just a place on the Council, but on the Symposium itself, the ruling body of the Connection.

Some Council members were missing from the semi-circle around me and a quick count confirmed that there were only nine witches present. The minimum number for the Council to be convened was seven, so we had some spares. Each witch sat with a cowl drawn up to shadow their face. The cowls were meant to offer anonymity and to intimidate. Abigay had told me that the Council didn't often meet with their cowls drawn up, yet here they were hidden by shadows. I couldn't help feeling they had more to hide than their faces.

Lights had been positioned so they shone directly into my eyes, and each chair had a lectern in front of it to provide a physical barrier. When I'd been here previously I'd felt vulnerable, but today I felt righteous and full of rage. Their petty psychological games had no effect on me.

I let the tense taut silence stretch until it was nearly agonising. My heartbeat was rushing in my ears, the only sound I could hear. And still, I let the moment drag on. This was their party and I'd be damned if I'd break first.

'How dare you bring a griffin into these chambers? We will be speaking to the golem about this outrage!' I recognised Jasper Ravenscroft's posh accent.

'You will *not.*' I bared my teeth. 'Benjamin Cohen is doing his job. He is aware that Bastion has been hired by the Council to protect me and he had no reason to refuse him entry.'

'Bastion is no longer retained by the Council,' another snotty voice said, 'not since you completed your—' snicker '—ORAL potion.' That was Seren; I knew her voice, cowl or not.

I tried not to reveal what a bombshell that was. If Bastion wasn't hired by the Council, then who *had* hired him? Oscar? And why the heck had he lied about it?

It was time to change the subject; I hadn't come here to talk about me. The best defence is a good offence. 'I'm not here to discuss my potion but to report a death. The Crone is dead,' I watched each witch in turn to see who looked shocked. Some hands flew to mouths hidden by the cowls; others held their hands to their hearts; others remained still.

'Murdered,' I added, in case that wasn't clear. I guessed Abigay was at an age when conceivably she could have died from natural causes. There were more gasps, but because of the cowls it was difficult to say who was truly shocked.

One voice, strong and unwavering but ripe with fury, spoke. 'What have you learned of the perpetrators?' Willow: I'd recognise her American accent anywhere.

'They used black mordis and they painted on a black rune that Council member Hilary Mitchell could not counter.'

'How did they get to the Crone? What of her wards?' Willow asked.

I shook my head, my frustration showing. 'The wards were intact.'

'Black magic,' Jasper spat.

'I am here to request permission to head an investigation into her death. I am motivated, and I happen to have a professional tracker working with me.' All eyes swung to Bastion.

'And what is your standing here?' Seren asked Bastion. 'You are no longer her bodyguard.'

'On the contrary, I am still retained to guard Miss De-Lea. The paymaster has changed but the job has not. Whether you will it or not, Amber will hunt down the Crone's killer so it is inevitable that I will face a black witch again.'

'That didn't turn out so well last time,' Tristan said snidely.

'Luckily I learn from my mistakes,' Bastion said mildly. The implication that Tristan did not was clear, and I struggled to keep a smirk from my face. I'd heard rumours – we all had – of the latest witch to catch Tristan's eye with a view to a seat on the Council; after all, it had worked for Seren.

'I request the use of the golem,' I continued.

'Why?' Seren huffed.

'He is made of white magic, so he is naturally immune to black magic. His whole purpose is to protect white witches; he would not – could not – take a bribe. If I want someone on my side that I can trust then it's Benjamin Cohen.'

'Agreed.' Willow spoke into the void. 'We can awaken the next golem to guard the Council's chamber. It is far more important to weed out this black witch – or witches – and if any here seeks to gainsay that, I'll be taking a hard look at you and your motivation.'

Rolling silence greeted the threat; tense glances were exchanged.

'There you have it,' Willow said lightly to me. 'Benjamin is your responsibility. He was made by thousands of hours of witchcraft. Do NOT break him.'

I resisted the urge to point out that his value was in his very being, his disposition and his smile, not the hours of witchcraft that it had taken to build him. I knew what it took; after all, I'd helped make him.

Chapter 14

Benji's delight at being free from the underground city made me smile, even with my aching heart. It had been a long time since he'd been above ground – years, at least. To the Common realmers, he would look like a large man 'built like a brick shit house'. But although his sheer bulk might make someone uneasy, it wouldn't set off alarm bells. He had the physique of a rugby player, nothing more.

Bastion had secured us rooms in a hotel called the Sheraton Grand, one of the best in Edinburgh. He had booked us a suite of rooms with interconnecting bedrooms, probably intending to use them to give him and me some space, but now the spare bedroom would be taken up by my newly appointed bodyguard, Benji.

When we arrived at the hotel, Bastion flashed a keycard and we took the lift up to the seventh floor. 'You have this room,' he instructed Benji, giving him the key to 724. 'We'll stay in this one,' he gestured to 725. 'Leave the interconnecting door unlocked in case of trouble.'

Benji nodded; he didn't seem to object to taking orders from a griffin. We went into our rooms. Bastion opened the interconnecting door, just to check it didn't open a portal to another dimension or something. Satisfied, he closed it again but didn't lock it.

I left the two men to explore their respective spaces and retreated into one of the bedrooms to make some calls. I had a number for Abigay's brother, Tarone, but it rang and rang until the answer machine clicked in. I hesitated. What if the Council hadn't notified him yet? In the end, I left a rather brusque message requesting a call back.

While I was making the call, Bastion joined me. I guessed it hadn't taken him long to explore and secure the small hotel suite.

I took my laptop out of my backpack and logged on to check on coven business. I was scrolling through my emails when a loud groan sounded through the wall. 'Benji!' I shouted in panic, tossing my laptop aside.

Bastion and I threw open the interconnecting door. Benji was sitting on the edge of his bed, studying his TV and frowning. Another moan rang out. I looked at the screen and flushed red from the top of my head to the tips of my toes. Goddess, how embarrassing.

Benji was watching porn, his expression mildly confused. 'Why would you lick there?' he asked, pointing.

I threw a panicked look to Bastion; I was *not* prepared to field this one. Bastion was out and out grinning. 'It's called oral sex,' he explained. 'Done properly, it's very enjoyable.'

'Oral?' Benji seized on the familiar word. 'Like Amber's potion?'

'Nothing like my potion!' I exclaimed quickly.

Bastion gave a full guffaw. I sent him a glare and that was it – he doubled over laughing. Benji watched him with mild concern. 'Is Bastion okay?'

'He finds it unfortunate that I named my potion the ORAL potion,' I said primly.

'I didn't know unfortunate things were funny.'

I glared at Bastion. 'They're not.' If anything, Bastion laughed harder.

The porn continued and more moans rang out. My cheeks couldn't get redder. 'I'll leave Bastion here with you to explain … things.'

I backed away and shut the door on the most mortifying experience of my life. I hustled back to my laptop and tried to lose myself in paperwork. It felt like ages before Bastion swaggered back in with a smile tugging at his lips. 'Did you explain the birds and the bees?' I asked, cheeks pink.

'Yup.'

'Goddess,' I muttered. Perhaps I should have listened in; I might have learnt a thing or two. Then again, given how many romance books I read ... probably not.

I put away my laptop, satisfied that Jeb, Ethan and Jacob had everything under control. They worked well as a team; none of them alone could run the coven in my absence, but together they did a great job. Jacob was doing the teaching, Ethan was running the roster and the potion store, and Jeb was picking up the slack with everything else. I almost felt a little ... unnecessary. I tossed the unhelpful thought aside and picked up my phone, planning to ring Oscar.

I hesitated as thoughts of Oscar's deception returned with full force. What was he keeping from me? My father's background? I hoped so because I'd had my fill of secrets. I prayed that his silence was at my mum's behest, and that it was the only snake in the grass. If he had another deep, dark secret then stick a fork in me – I was done.

I dialled before I could talk myself out of it and Oscar answered on the second ring. 'Amber. Are you okay?'

I felt a twinge of guilt at the stress I was putting him under. He wasn't getting any younger. 'I'm okay. The potion?'

'I have been unable to meet with the seer,' he admitted, sounding annoyed.

'Melva?'

'Indeed. I am told that her diary is full.'

Damn Nell, her dragon-like secretary. 'Who else have you tried to see?'

Oscar rattled off a list of seers. Rune ruin! I bit my lip. 'Ring Meredith to see what she wants to do. If we wait much longer to administer the antidote, it will lose its efficacy.'

'Are you suggesting we give Ria an untested potion?' His tone was shocked.

'If we don't, she'll be on a countdown to death anyway,' I said, matter-of-factly.

'But this could hasten it,' Oscar argued.

'It won't.'

'You don't know that.'

'I am ninety-five percent certain. Tell Meredith that and let her make her choice.'

'Fine,' he responded brusquely. He paused for a moment before he spoke again. 'Abigay?'

'Dead.'

I heard a sharp, indrawn breath, 'I'm sorry,' he murmured. His own voice was suddenly thick and I realised I was being a complete douche. He had known Abigay nearly as long as I had, and he didn't deserve to hear such news delivered in such a blunt way. What was wrong with me?

'I'm sorry.' I repeated his words, rubbing my forehead in consternation. 'I'm not myself.' I was frequently without tact but not this bad; I was off my game. Seeing Abigay die... I would never forget it.

Oscar didn't respond for such a long time that I wondered whether he'd hung up. 'Shall I tell Luna?' he asked finally. His voice caught and I realised he'd been crying soundlessly. Now I really felt awful.

'See what kind of day it is,' I advised finally.

'Okay. I'll see to Ria first. Goodbye.' He hung up abruptly and my conscience pricked uncomfortably. I had royally ballsed that up.

The Council wasted no time in arranging Abigay's funeral; she was dead and on a pyre on the same day.

The cold air whipped around us, even through the heavy cloak I had wrapped around me. I ducked under the tape, noting the explanation given to the Common realm for tonight's spectacle. *Restricted access: Film Set,* it claimed.

Numerous wizard security guards stood at points around the cordon and most of them gave me a nod of recognition. I inclined my head to return their greetings. I had chosen not to wear my cowl up tonight and had let my red hair tumble down my back like a fiery beacon. *Come for me,* I dared the black witches.

Benji and Bastion were either side of me; both were tense and ready for trouble. Good. I was looking for it.

I had approached Calton Hill from the steps off Regent Road, another reminder that I was not as fit as I should be. My legs burned but I was unsure whether it was from the number of steps or being astride Bastion for so many hours. If I was making it my life's work to hunt down black witches, I should probably add some cardio and weapon training to my life. I was a brilliant rune master, healer and potioneer, but I was significantly worse at hand-to-hand combat. And I wouldn't always be able to rely on others to fight my battles for me.

I had another potion bomb in my pocket; I'd taken Abigay's from her bedside drawer. It was a valuable defensive potion, incredibly expensive to produce and even harder to brew, but I knew she wouldn't begrudge me it. I'd made it once myself and then never again; it had taken nearly thirty-six hours of straight brewing, and one mistake wouldn't cost you just the potion but also your life. There were only a handful of licensed brewers for this particular potion in the world.

In front of the twelve columns of Calton Hill lay a pyre. It had been built high and Abigay's still form was on top of it, wrapped in white linen and doused in a flammable potion. Darkness had fallen and we gathered in heavy mournful silence. Around us flickered oil torches that had been thrust into the ground. The crackle of the flames was all that broke the quivering quiet that had settled upon us all. My heart was racing. This was the moment. The aching acknowledgement of all that the Crone had been and done. We stood on this hallowed ground and we grieved as one.

The coven of witches stood still and silent. There would be no pretty words, no flowery eulogy. The Crone was a role that demanded a total loss of identity. Those gathered here were not mourning Abigay the person that I loved, but the loss of the Crone and the stability of a full triune.

We waited in the flickering flames for the ceremony to begin. The mournful wail of a bagpipe rose. When I heard the first drumbeat, the tension in my shoulders loosened. The next drummer joined in and then the next and then the next, until the cacophony was almost deafening. My blood quickened in answer to the ancient beat but my eyes remained dry. This wasn't the time for mourning now; that wasn't what the drumbeat was for. Someone had killed the Crone and it was an attack on us all. The fire would warn our enemies that their deaths were coming in turn. There would be no reprisals for the person who killed the Crone's murderer. It was open season.

One of the torchbearers stepped forward and touched his flame to the pyre. The fire took hold instantly and soon the heat of it had us all yearning to step back. But we stood, almost burning in the blaze, letting the light of Abigay's fire shine out over Edinburgh.

And still the drums beat.

It wasn't a lament but a call to war.

Chapter 15

I remained dry-eyed even as my fellow witches touched my arm in sympathy. My friendship with Abigay had been well known. I nodded sharply; no doubt I appeared cold, but if I'd opened my mouth to thank them a sob would have ripped out, and I was *not* crying on Calton Hill. Instead I looked around me, at my cloaked brothers and sisters, and wondered which one had killed Abigay. That thought kept the beat of the drums in my heart.

When the pyre had burned down and the music had stopped, people started to leave. Benji reached out and tugged my hand, 'We should go, Am. It's not safe for you here.'

Where is? I wanted to ask, but despair isn't pretty so I stayed silent.

It felt like I was always reacting to things that were happening around me, but now I wanted to take the fight to them, the black coven. Even thinking their name made me shudder. They were part of a bogeyman story to tell the coven kids – or rather they had been. Now I knew they were real.

Black coven be damned; I would find Abigay's killer and I would see them dead. I didn't even feel bad about that thought. My blood was hot and angry, burning in my veins. I wanted vengeance and more – I wanted to make sure this never happened again. And the only way to do that was to destroy the whole damned black coven.

I let Benji lead me away with Bastion hot on my heels. We could have caught a tram but I was in the mood to walk so we strode along Princes Street. Even in the darkness I could see the cherry trees in full bloom. Abigay had loved walking along this road with its monuments to the left and right. The Scots believe in honouring their dead and statues and obelisks had been raised to commemorate those who deserved remembering – or the rich. Sometimes even both.

The city was even more beautiful in the dark of the night. The castle dominated the skyline, reminding all who saw it of times gone by when fortifications and ramparts had been a part of ordinary life. It felt like those times were returning.

'This way.' Benji tugged my arm as we crossed the final square. The Sheraton Grand was a modern building but only a stone's throw away was the Usher Hall with its domed ceiling and ornate décor. Edinburgh is a city that stylishly and effortlessly mixes the old and the new in a smorgasbord of culture. It is one of my favourite cities, but at that moment it reminded me too sharply of Abigay. She'd lived and died here and now it would forever hold memories of her.

We flashed our keycards to get into our rooms and said good night to Benji. Despite the late hour I needed something to do, so I climbed into the shower. I could hear Bastion moving around and muttering but I blocked him out. I needed to wash the smoke from my hair.

I felt numb as I scrubbed the day from me – I was in shock or denial or something. It was hard to know what was wrong, save for the fact that my heart ached.

I dried myself mechanically and slid into pyjamas. I couldn't be bothered to dry my hair, so I left it wet and limp. When I came out of the bathroom, Bastion had made me a cup of tea. The hotel mug was entirely too small for my needs but it would have to do. He'd switched on the TV.

COVEN OF THE WITCH

'What's that?' I asked, gesturing to the screen that he'd paused when I came in.

'A movie.'

'No, really?' I let sarcasm colour my tone and a faint smile curved his lips in response.

'Sit.' He pointed to the edge of the king-size bed.

I sat. He straightened some cushions, shuffled onto the bed behind me and pressed play. Then, to my surprise, he took my hair and started to segment it and brush it.

The film began: *The Notebook*. The soft, sad strains of a song began whilst someone rowed across a lake at sunset. Something about the beauty of the scene struck a chord with me and a rock lodged in my throat. I realised I was going to cry before the damned thing had even started.

I watched, wholly consumed by the beautiful love story of Nick and Allie. I was completely undone by Allie suffering from dementia, a disease I knew all too well. Allie's illness was so complete that she had no memory of her past. That was a fear I battled every day with Mum, that soon there wouldn't be good days and bad days, only bad days. Then she would be lost to me forever whilst she was still here on Earth beside me.

I sobbed my heart out. I cried and cried for Abigay, for Mum and for myself.

Chapter 16

When I awoke and checked the time, I saw that I had a text message from Oscar. *Ria took the antidote, the black veins have disappeared but she hasn't regained consciousness yet.* It had been sent at 6am, my usual waking time. Because of my late night and my crying jag, I'd slept until the rather ridiculous time of 10am. Bastion had ordered us room service: a full Scottish breakfast for him and Benji, and scrambled eggs and smoked salmon for me.

Benji attacked his breakfast with enthusiasm. 'They usually give me gruel,' he confessed with a happy smile as he sipped his orange juice. Fury crackled in my veins; when I had a seat on the Council, the first thing I'd do was overhaul golem rights.

I sipped my tea to calm myself. Somehow Bastion had managed to replace my crappy hotel mug with a far larger one which simply had the Scottish flag on it. He had seen my disdainful sniff at the size of the hotel's mugs and he or Benji must have visited a souvenir shop bright and early.

'Thank you,' I murmured, gesturing to the mug. Benji looked baffled, which answered the question of who had bought the mug for me.

As always, Bastion barely acknowledged my thanks. 'What's the plan?' he asked instead.

'We're going to find out who killed Abigay.'

He considered. 'We already know the method of death – black mordis – but we need to ascertain motive and opportunity.'

'Unfortunately virtually every witch in Edinburgh had the opportunity. The Crone had an open-door policy. Any witch could get an appointment to see her, though we'd need her stolen diary to find out exactly who she was due to meet.'

'Even so, The Witchery will have CCTV footage. We'll be able to see who comes and goes.'

'Yes, but the CCTV only covers access to the restaurant. Unfortunately the accommodation side of the building doesn't have any.'

Bastion grimaced. 'It's still a starting point.'

'I agree.' Which is why, half an hour later, all three of us were ensconced in the back room of The Witchery watching grainy CCTV footage.

'Stop!' I called, frowning. 'That's Abigay's brother, Tarone Morgan. I'm ninety percent sure it's him.' What the hell was Tarone doing in Edinburgh? And if he was here, why hadn't he shown up at her funeral pyre?

I hauled out my phone and left him another terse voice-mail – this time requesting a meet as soon as possible.

We continued to watch the footage. There were a number of people besides Hilary who'd come cloaked and hooded. 'This has been a waste of time,' I grumped. 'Those hooded people could be anyone.'

Bastion disagreed. 'We spotted Tarone, so that's something. What's their relationship like?'

'Acrimonious. Tarone wanted Abigay to marry and stay in Jamaica to raise a brood of children to continue the Morgan line. She didn't want to – she claimed she didn't have a maternal bone in her body.' Much like me.

'She moved here at least partly for her freedom,' I went on. 'Her parents died when she was relatively young and Tarone took over managing the family. He kept the reins tight, tried to dictate whom she dated and which coven she belonged to. She got out from under his thumb by escaping in the dead of night. By the time he found her in England, she'd already established herself as a witch of some repute. She had friends in high places and allies who could be dangerous.' My mum had been both the former and the latter.

'He let her stay?'

'There wasn't much "letting" involved. He told her to come home, she said no – with a cadre of badass witches behind her, including my mum and Hilary – and he flounced back to Jamaica.'

'Would that have angered him enough to kill her?' Benji asked.

I wrinkled my nose. 'If it had, he'd have done it twenty years ago. Not now.' Unless he believed in serving vengeance cold – twenty years cold.

'And yet he was seen entering The Witchery and soon afterwards Abigay was dead,' Bastion pointed out.

Hard to argue with that logic. 'He's a person of interest,' I agreed. 'Let's see if we can nail down a location for him by normal means. If not, I'll try to scry him.'

'We don't have anything belonging to him,' Bastion said.

Damn him for being right. 'Then you'd best find him, hadn't you? You're a tracker – go track.'

His lips twitched. 'Yes, ma'am, but only when you're safely back in the hotel.'

As Benji rose to stretch his legs, my phone beeped again with a message from my clinic secretary, Janice: *All green for tonight?*

Shit. I had forgotten about the clinic. I rubbed a hand over my forehead. Well, at least I'd had a lie-in and I'd still be good to go later. *All green.* I confirmed. Now I just had to get from Edinburgh to Slough by 9pm.

'Why are you frowning?' Bastion asked.

'I have a clinic tonight,' I murmured, low enough so that Benji wouldn't hear. He's a golem and, as such, his loyalty is to the coven Council whether he wishes it or not. His free will is tightly constrained by rules and regulations – and healing for free is a big no-no. If he found out what I was doing, he'd be duty-bound to report it.

Bastion followed my gaze to where Benji was happily taking some more sausages and understanding lit his eyes. 'We can leave him here searching for Tarone while we get a helicopter home for "a coven emergency".'

I hated lying to Benji but it was the lesser of two evils. Telling him about the clinic would put him in an invidious position, so it was for his own good. 'Okay. Arrange the helicopter,' I murmured.

I texted Peter Glenn, a potion ingredient grower whom I'd met once at his request. He grows a plethora of exotic flora and fauna at the Palm House in Liverpool. Black mordis kept coming up time and time again. Its ingredients were common – bar the last one. *Someone has been brewing black mordis. Have you sold any felfa leaves recently?*

He responded almost instantly. *I am very careful who I sell felfa to. No one of late.*

Can you make enquiries with other growers?

It will be difficult. No one will want to disrupt the status quo.

Black mordis, I replied simply. It is the most deadly potion that has ever been made. Felfa is an ingredient in other potions, too; if it is sliced and not boiled then it can be consumed, but if it is crushed... A lick of magic will activate the deadly toxins and compound the potential for murder.

I will ask, Peter responded simply.

That was all I could do. It might be that this area of investigation would hit a brick wall but at least I'd done everything I could. Not for the first time I wished I had the skill to compel someone to tell me the truth just by looking at them. Drawing truth runes takes an unholy amount of time, and even then you have to get your intended victim to stand or sit on them while they are activated.

While my phone was out, I texted Oscar and told him about the clinic. If Meredith and Ria were okay to be left alone, he could meet me there. And afterwards, I planned to have words with him about my father.

Chapter 17

Bastion gave Benji a list of places where Tarone had spent money during the past week and asked him to use his contacts to track down Tarone's whereabouts so that we could confront him. Bastion made it clear that Benji should not approach Tarone without us.

Benji nodded solemnly, his chest puffed with pride at the importance of the task laid on him.

For some reason, I couldn't shake the feeling that Tarone wasn't the killer. As I'd said to the men, if he'd wanted Abigay dead he could have killed her years earlier. And Abigay had told me that he was a stickler for rules and tradition; everything was black and white to him. From what she'd said, black magic was repugnant to him. I could see him attacking his sister with *angrepet* – a dagger – but not a black rune. Still, people change. He was on the suspect list, meagre though it was.

Before I went to the clinic, I stole down to the underground city with my bodyguards in tow. I wanted to talk to Eleanora Moonspell, who was also on the suspect list. Eleanora pretty much ran the underground market and she'd earned a huge amount of respect and goodwill in the community. If I had to put money on who would be the next Crone, it would be her or Hilary. People had killed for far less.

I let the dank chill wash over me. Benji gave a happy hum and wiggled his shoulders; I guess the coolness agreed with him because it was all he'd known for a very long time. He held out a hand to stop me from moving forward. 'I'll go ahead and scout out the market. Wait here.'

He didn't wait for me to agree before his clay form rolled over his clothes, subsuming them until he stood naked. Golems aren't anatomically correct; although he was male in nature, he was not – well, male in *nature*.

He stepped forward and disappeared into the walls and my mouth dropped open. I'd had no idea he could do that. He had been made by dozens of acolytes and witches working together, but I'd never seen any runework that would enable him to become one with the walls. Was he becoming part of the walls, or was he merely travelling through them?

COVEN OF THE WITCH

'Neat trick,' Bastion commented.

'Did you know he could do that?' I asked, aghast. *I* hadn't known that and I'd helped to make him.

Bastion shook his head. 'No, but it could definitely come in handy.'

We waited in silence. Bastion was visibly edgy and his hand was floating near a blade on his hip. I guessed cold steel was his equivalent of a safety blanket, though it was equally unnecessary; I'd seen Bastion perform a partial shift and transform his hands into talons that were ready to rip out throats effortlessly, so a knife was somewhat superfluous. Though, as he'd said, he couldn't throw his claws so maybe it wasn't *totally* superfluous.

'Okay.' Benji's distorted voice came from the walls themselves. I glanced around but I couldn't see him. 'I've checked and there are definitely no ogres in the under-ground city. The market is all clear.'

He stepped out of the walls, concentrated for a moment and brought his black suit forward again. It was immaculate, without even a hint of the clay that should have covered it. 'That is so cool,' I said. Mindful of his need for human contact, I gave him a smile and a pat on the arm.

He grinned broadly. 'I've got some skills, Am.'

'Of that I have no doubt, my friend.'

Benji took point and led us to the underground market. Bastion stayed at the rear, still vibrating with tension, his eyes jerking this way and that, constantly assessing everything around us for a potential threat. It must have been exhausting.

The market was unusually busy. Stalls lined the square courtyard but groups of witches were huddled drinking tea and coffee from the pop-up café. Everyone wanted to be together, to have the feeling of community. There was safety in numbers – or so they assumed. Safety was illusory, I thought, as I fingered the potion bomb in my pocket.

I spotted Eleanora Moonspell at the main potions stall and made my way to her. Her warm, welcoming smile disappeared the instant that she saw me approaching and she grimaced. Always nice to have a fan. She stepped aside and tapped her assistant on the shoulder to tell him to take over the stall whilst she dealt with me.

'Moonspell,' I greeted her coolly.

'DeLea,' she responded just as glacially. 'I suppose it's no surprise to see you here.'

'And why is that?'

She snorted. 'Everyone knows that you're investigating who killed the Crone.'

'And why should that bring me to your door?' I asked, raising an eyebrow.

'Because I'm going to be the next Crone,' she asserted confidently. 'Hilary and Beatrice might think that they're in with a shot but they're not. They are Council members and the Council will want them to stay there. It will be far easier to replace the Crone with someone from outside the Council than to recruit more Council members, especially when we are already down one Symposium member. Look how long it's taken them to do anything about that! It's just logistics.'

She folded her arms. 'Regardless of that, I would never have killed to obtain the position. Whatever you think of me, you must know that. Like you, potions have been a huge part of my life's work but I have never taken a shortcut. I believe in working for what you want to attain.'

I didn't quite follow her logic about the hiring policy. Either way, someone would have to be recruited either to be the Crone or to be a replacement Council member. I didn't see the point in arguing with her, however; there was a more pressing question. 'And what if what *you* want to attain is the Crone's position?'

She leaned forward. 'Then I would have cemented a position in the market, made myself invaluable to the community and waited for the current Crone to die.' She rolled her eyes. 'Of natural causes,' she clarified hastily. 'You can look at me as hard as you want, but it's a waste of your time and mine. Abigay and I had our differences but we both had the interests of the witch community at heart.'

Of that I had no doubt – but was it the best interests of the witch community or the *black* witch community? 'Did you go to the ceilidh the night before Abigay died?'

She frowned at my line of questioning. 'Yes, but Abigay didn't come.'

'Who did?'

She snorted, 'Better to ask who didn't. All the movers and shakers were there bar Abigay and Hilary. They sat drinking together in The Witchery rather than socialising with the rest of us.' She sniffed. 'But the rest of the Council were there. I should know because I spent most of the night talking with them.'

'Trying to secure the Crone position?'

She glared. 'No, the Crone position wasn't vacant then. I was trying to get an invitation to be tested for membership of the Symposium.' Dammit, that was *my* role. The last thing I needed was Moonspell throwing her hat into the ring. Kassandra was good competition but Moonspell would be damned hard to beat and, like me, she'd worked hard to build a reputation and a solid base of allies.

'If it wasn't you who killed Abigay,' I asked baldly, 'then who was it?' I needed more suspects. Moonspell wasn't off the list but she was further down than she had been before we'd had this chat.

She gave a one-shouldered shrug. 'I'd look harder at Hilary and Beatrice.'

'You said it yourself – they're less likely to become the Crone than you are,' I argued.

'Yes, but they don't know that. They're delusional and they think that their seats on the Council are an advantage. They're completely wrong, of course. I've spent years doing hard graft, serving the community. I'm the obvious choice.'

'And if you don't get invited?'

She threw up her hands. 'Well then obviously I'm going to bomb the world,' she huffed sarcastically. 'If I don't get the position I'll try again when the next Crone dies, and I'll set my sights on a position on the Council in the meantime. Failing that, maybe it's time for me to become a Coven Mother. I have plenty of avenues open to me, but all I know is that I'm done peddling wares in the underground market. I want to see some damned daylight, not to mention that I'm getting too old for the long hours the market requires. I want a *cushy* job.'

I thought of Abigay's role – becoming the Crone, losing her name, serving the Goddess's whims. It wasn't a cushy job; it was a difficult one. I'd always thought that Eleanora Moonspell would be a good Crone but now I had my doubts. If she was looking for the path of least resistance, then the Crone's path wouldn't be for her. I knew from Abigay how hard the job was. She had constantly travelled up and down the country, sorting out disputes within the covens that the Coven Mothers couldn't resolve. And she consulted the stars and the Goddess for the best direction to guide the Council to maximise the witches' success in the future.

No: the Crone's job was a lot of things but cushy wasn't one of them. As it had turned out, it was also pretty deadly.

Chapter 18

I left Edinburgh very reluctantly. Bastion had sourced us a helicopter so at least we didn't have to use Griffin Air again or spend six hours driving back down south. I hated leaving Benji, although he was far from vulnerable. He hadn't been above the surface all that much, and the outside world was fast-paced and violent. He was still a little naïve and I honestly wanted to keep him that way. It was part of his charm.

I didn't want to cart Grimmy up and down the country, nor did I want to leave him in a hotel, so I gave my bag to Benji and explained that it held something very dear to me. Shocked, I watched Benji lift his shirt and push the bag into his clay body. His shape was distorted for a moment then it rippled as it redistributed itself and he became an inch or two taller. Cool.

I gave him a big hug before boarding the helicopter and he promised me that he would be careful. That would have to suffice. I felt a bit like a proud mother letting my child loose upon the world; creating Benji was probably the closest I'd come to motherhood, but now he was far more than the runes that I had once painted painstakingly onto his prone form.

Once we were in the helicopter, Bastion surprised me by pulling out another book. This one was entitled *Fiery Waters* and the blurb told me that it was a forbidden romance story between a fire elemental and a water elemental. I thanked him and took it happily. The stress of the day melted away as I lost myself in Jack and Sam's love story.

I felt rejuvenated when the helicopter set us down in a park in Slough. Onlookers were gaping at us – helicopters weren't common fare. Bastion and I hustled away as it took off again to pick up its next commercial hire.

The clinic was only a few streets away but the walk there was incredibly tense. The area wasn't the best, night had fallen and someone was trying to kill me, as evidenced by the fire elemental flinging fireballs at me … so it was stressful. And worse, because I'd come from Edinburgh, I had none of my stuff with me. Luckily, I spotted Oscar parked outside the clinic. I headed hastily for the car and he slid out, his arms full of my cloak and tote bag, no doubt packed to the brim with potions and paintbrushes. I threw myself into his arms.

'I'm sorry,' I murmured. Sorry for Abigay's death, sorry for telling him about it so bluntly, sorry for leaving him behind. My world righted a little as he awkwardly patted my back. I felt so much better for having him by my side. I clung to him for a moment longer, letting him know with actions what I couldn't say with words.

Finally I stepped back and cleared my throat awkwardly. 'How is Ria?' I kept my voice low.

He smiled. 'She's good. Much better. She came round this morning. She's going to be okay.'

I let out an explosive breath as more tension left me. Thank the Goddess for that.

'Meredith wants her somewhere safe, away from the black coven's eyes. The Circus?' Oscar murmured, mindful of Bastion's presence a few feet away. Bastion wasn't paying us any attention, though; he was scrutinising the shadows around us.

I nodded slowly. 'Yes, good idea. Hopefully it will only be a temporary relocation. Call Cain.'

Oscar nodded briskly. 'I will.' He held out my cloak and I slipped it on and pulled up the cowl. I shivered as the seer-bespelled article cast mysterious shadows across my face to keep me hidden from sight. I shouldered my tote bag and entered the clinic with Bastion on my heels.

The creatures that waited there visibly recoiled at the sight of my griffin protector; Bastion was well-known even in his human form. The moniker 'deadliest assassin' sure came with a wallop of judgement. Not that I could throw stones: I'd judged him plenty before I knew him. Now I knew that he was warm, kind – and unafraid to buy me romance books. He was also keeping a secret from me, but that was for another day. My mind had enough to whirr over. Abigay had to be my focus – well, Abigay and the clinic.

I looked around the waiting room and mentally triaged the visible injuries. Without a doubt, the worst was the imp sitting on Tobias's lap. Perhaps the dragon shifter and owner of the Court Curiosities shop really had flown him here. I'd last seen Tobias in his shop in Edinburgh. The dragon had a hand in every pie and he'd helped me secure an essential ingredient for my ORAL potion. I owed him, and I guess the imp on his lap was going to reap the benefits of that.

Like Frogmatch, the imp whose tail I'd healed a few weeks earlier, Brambleford's tail had also been severed, but unlike Frogmatch it hadn't been done recently. Bramble-ford looked like he was one breath away from death. I had no idea how long he'd been missing his tail but it had been too long and I wasn't sure if I could save him.

Tobias's eyes widened at the sight of Bastion then his eyes swept over to me. Realisation in his eyes. I was busted; he knew I was Ellie. Dammit, I should have hidden Bastion somehow. Regardless, I had no time to worry about that now. Brambleford needed me.

I went into my office and prepared myself. 'Did you see the imp?' I asked Bastion.

He nodded. Of course he had; he missed nothing.

'The tail was cut off but it looks like it happened a few weeks ago. If the tail has healed too much, I won't be able to regrow it.'

Bastion studied me. 'Unless a fresh wound appears.'

Thank goodness he was sharp. 'Exactly.'

'You want me to chop off a little more tail.'

'I need to know if it's an option.' He nodded once in acquiescence. 'Thank you.' Relief rushed through me. Without Bastion's help, I would have had to chop off more of the tail and the mere thought made me turn green. I'm good at healing injuries but not so good at inflicting them – except for barbecuing rogue fire elementals. I shoved the thought aside before horror overwhelmed me. I'd deal with that episode another day.

I told Janice to send in Brambleford. Tobias entered, carrying him in his hands. The red-skinned imp was so pale he looked almost pink, and he could barely stand. I worried that his heart wouldn't take Bastion's slicing and dicing, and chided myself for not healing him there and then when Tobias had asked for me to set up an appointment with 'Ellie'. Now Brambleford might be dying just to protect my identity. It wasn't worth it, dammit.

I set up the desk with my lamp and magnifying glass. 'Hello,' I greeted Brambleford gently. 'Your tail was removed. Was it by a vampire?'

He looked startled. 'Yes, how did you know?'

'You're not the first imp to come to the clinic,' I said grimly. I wondered how many *hadn't* made it here. I'd sent the image of the vampyr to Lord Wokeshire, but I didn't know if the culprit had been caught. Anger stirred in my gut and I had to push it down to do my job.

'I got enchanted by a vampyr,' he said in angry helplessness. 'It shouldn't be possible. They can't normally enchant us.'

I frowned but that was a mystery for another day. He was a heartbeat away from death, and I had no time to concern myself with anything other than saving his life. 'Your tail has already healed,' I started, 'so I can't re-grow it as it is.'

A single tear ran down Brambleford's face as all hope drained out of him.

'But if it is cut again,' I added hastily, 'we can try and heal it. We need a wound to work with. Obviously I need your permission for that, and there is a risk that the pain and shock will kill you.'

He trembled. 'Without my tail, I'm dead anyway. Do it, witch. Chop me up.'

I met Bastion's eyes and jerked my head towards the table. Bastion was ready – as always – and his hands had already shifted into talons. The claws glinted, sharp and deadly, and the imp whimpered. I didn't blame him one bit; if Bastion came at me with those claws, I'd pee myself. My pelvic floor isn't what it once was, yet another indignity of ageing. Better than the alternative though, I suppose.

I held the imp's tail and Bastion brought his claws down with a surgeon's precision. Only the tiniest slice of skin fell away but blood immediately started to gush. The imp gave a bloodcurdling scream then promptly passed out. I started painting in earnest.

I was going to save this little imp, and then I was going to sic Bastion on the vampyr that had dared to rip off his tail.

Chapter 19

There was exhaustion in every line of my body and my skin was itching like mad. Luckily Oscar knew how long it was since I'd last visited a portal and he'd sneaked a vial of my ORAL potion into my tote bag.

I unstoppered the glass vial of Other Realm Additional Length potion and downed it in one. The itching vanished immediately and a flood of magic filled me. It was the best damned thing I'd ever made.

As I wiped down the surfaces in the surgery, the routine task soothed me and cleared my buzzing mind. Tired as I was, I couldn't switch off, couldn't stop replaying the moment of Abigay's death and wondering if I could have done something to save her. Tonight I'd saved three lives; three people – including Brambleford – would have died if it hadn't been for me. Yet I hadn't saved Abigay.

'Whatever you're telling yourself,' Bastion growled, 'stop it.'

I put my hands on my hips and narrowed my eyes at the exasperating griffin. 'Oh, so now even my thoughts are censored, are they?'

'You're beating yourself up. You saved lives tonight, you've made a difference, and it's still not good enough for you. What *will* be good enough for you, Amber?'

That was a valid question. Mum had raised me to push for success, to work hard to achieve my maximum potential – but how would I know when I'd reached it? I rubbed my tired eyes. What would be enough? If I kept moving the goal posts, would I ever know happiness? Maybe happiness was for others.

I toyed with my phone and contemplated ringing Lucy – she knew a little about happiness – but it was late. Very late. So instead I shook my head and let the argument die.

We left the clinic with Bastion wrapped around me like the bacon in a pig-in-blanket. 'Worried about a sniper?' I asked drily.

'I worry about everything. That's my job.'

I swallowed the retort that usually his job was at the other end of the rifle, but he read my expression. 'Yeah, yeah,' he breathed, his tone exasperated. 'I'm evil, etc.'

I stopped abruptly and touched his arm. 'I don't think you're evil.' I was surprised at how true that was. 'You're a good man.'

Surprise flashed across his face, there and gone in an instant before his impassive mask was resumed. He didn't respond. Pushing the small of my back to get me moving again, he hustled me into the relative safety of the car.

Oscar took one look at my face and, reading the tiredness there, passed us our food. Chinese takeout: delicious. The car roared to life while Bastion and I chowed down.

We were only a few streets away from home when Oscar cleared his throat. 'We have a tail,' he announced. 'It's been following us for the last three turns.'

Bastion swore quietly and looked surreptitiously in the rear-view mirror. 'The Mondeo?' Oscar nodded.

It was nearly 2am and we were virtually the only ones on the road. That was why it was so surprising when a truck trundled out of a side road and barrelled towards us at speed. 'Step on it!' Bastion yelled to Oscar as he shifted. He threw himself at me, his body and wings wrapping around me protectively.

Oscar did indeed step on it and the car lurched forward just in time. The huge truck struck us in the rear, sending us spinning wildly down the road until we collided with a lamppost and came to an abrupt stop.

Bastion had been wrapped around me but I'd looked up at just the wrong time; at the moment of impact, my head had slammed into the window. It hurt and I felt woozy. Curiosity killed the witch, I thought ruefully, or at least gave her concussion.

'Stay in the car!' Bastion growled then he left me – to go and kill our assailants, no doubt. I heard grunts and shouts and my brain finally started to fire again. I pushed myself up, fumbling with the seatbelt. My tote bag had been slammed against the car and it was now full of broken glass and a miasma of dangerously mixed potions. I opened it, selected a huge shard as a weapon then closed it again.

I opened my door and stumbled out into a battle-ground. Oscar wasn't in the car; he was using the IR – the intention and release – to amplify the flames from his lighter. He was wielding it like a blowtorch. The scent of crispy chicken filled the air.

There were three unmoving bodies on the ground – ogres – but four of them were still moving. One was focused on Oscar, dodging his fire like a ballerina, and three were on Bastion.

'Incoming!' I called to Bastion. I trickled my magic into the potion bomb in my pocket, hauled it out and threw it. I aimed for the pavement in front of them – so naturally it struck one of the ogres in the eye. It exploded on contact and threw them all back, except Bastion who'd backed away the instant I'd warned him.

Two ogres lay unmoving; one still twitched a little.

I turned to check on Oscar. He was frowning at the ogre that was still dancing around him swinging his mace dangerously close. I unzipped my tote bag and threw it towards the ogre. 'Catch!' I shouted.

Instinct made him do exactly that. As he caught the bag, the mix of potions and glass spewed out of the opening. He laughed at the little shards. 'These won't hurt me, little girl.'

I glared at him. I was forty-two. Did he need to be so patronising? 'No,' I agreed calmly as Oscar threw his flames again. They caught the potions that were liberally sprayed over the ogre and he lit up like a bonfire. 'But that might,' I pointed out drily. His screams were quite horrific and Bastion kindly put an end to them by slicing his throat.

Behind him, the last twitching ogre struggled to his feet. 'Behind you!' I warned Bastion urgently.

He turned on his heel, sauntered over to the struggling ogre and effortlessly pushed him back down. 'Know when you're done,' he advised sagely. 'All your compatriots are dead, each and every one of them. I suggest you get busy leaving or get busy dying. Your choice.' His tone was light and conversational; this was business as usual for Bastion.

The ogre lurched to his feet and stumbled away.

'Compassion, Bastion? Isn't that a little out of character?' Oscar snarked. He flicked his lighter closed and pocketed it. Before all this, I'd never seen Oscar kill so much as a spider, yet he'd flambéed the attacking ogres without hesitation. Obviously I knew he'd been hired as a driver *and* a bodyguard, but seeing his skills in action was something else.

'No,' I sighed. 'It's not. He's a big marshmallow softie.' After all, Bastion was the type of guy who'd sleep on a hardwood floor to reassure a girl that there were no monsters under her bed.

'Shush,' Bastion chastened. 'No one can know.'

That dragged a smile from me. 'That ogre might know,' I pointed out.

'Nah. You always leave one survivor. That way they can spread the news of your deadly skills.' He winked at me.

'Ah, of course. No point questioning the survivor, I suppose?' I made it a question but we both knew the answer. The ogres would never betray their contract. If they knew who their employer was, which was doubtful, they'd rather die than tell us.

'No,' Bastion agreed laconically.

The silver lining was that we'd survived another attack, and I was grateful for that. But I was starting to get really pissed off. It was time to take some decisive action of my own.

Chapter 20

The site of the car 'accident' was just around the corner from the coven, so it didn't take Jeb long to come out with the coven's van. At my request, Bastion and Oscar loaded up the ogres' bodies. Then, due to the limited seating in the front of the van, Bastion and I drove off leaving Oscar and Jeb to walk back to the coven tower.

'Should you be driving?' Bastion asked levelly. 'You hit your head pretty hard.'

'I had Jeb bring me a potion. He runed me while you guys were loading up the bodies.'

He was quiet for a moment. 'I know Jeb likes you, but doesn't it worry you? Letting a witch rune you when there are so many black witches running around?'

I blinked; that thought hadn't even occurred to me. I trusted Jeb. Dammit – maybe I *shouldn't* trust Jeb. 'He runed me on my arm,' I said finally. 'I could see every rune he drew. It was all above board.'

Bastion relaxed a little. 'Okay. Where are we going?'

'Where do you think we're going?'

'To a crematorium?'

I shook my head. The coven's cremator could have done the job, if that had been what I wanted to do. I drove purposefully. As we approached Beaconsfield, I saw Bastion's eyes narrow. 'You are *not* driving us to Krieg,' he said firmly.

'No?' I said mildly. Because I absolutely was. High King Robert Krieg was the king of the ogres. He lived in a chocolate box cottage at the edge of the town set in an acre of beautiful grounds complete with a lake and lots of trees for his murder of crows.

Bastion swore darkly and closed his eyes for a moment. When he opened them, they were gold. 'What's with the eagle eyes?' I asked.

'I summoned Raven.'

'Fehu?'

He snorted. 'Yes, your Fehu.' He paused. 'He likes having a proper name,' he admitted ruefully.

'I should think so! Poor bird. You've been calling him Raven this whole time.'

'It's what he is.'

'Shall I call you Griffin, then?'

He shrugged like he didn't care what I called him and I grinned. I wondered how long it would take him to ask me to call him Bastion again. I'd give him a day.

'Going to Krieg is a bad idea.' He was back on topic.

'You went to see him with Lucy,' I pointed out. I didn't like the way my gut twisted at the thought that he somehow trusted her more than me.

'Yes – and that was an equally bad idea.'

'You're both alive, so it wasn't *that* bad an idea,' I pointed out.

He ignored that. 'What do you know of their customs?'

'Enough.'

Bastion touched my upper arm lightly, just the barest touch before he retreated again. He was willing me to take him seriously. 'This isn't a joke. You are strolling into their den and they have been hired to kill you. The chances of us walking out alive are miniscule. This is a *bad* idea, a *very bad* idea.' I huffed. 'You need to take this seriously,' he growled.

'Have I ever given you the impression that I'm not serious?' I asked quietly.

'No,' he admitted.

'Then trust me.'

I parked outside the cutesy-wootsy cottage, opened the back of the van and pulled one of the dead ogres by the feet. 'Help me,' I instructed Bastion.

He grabbed the heavy body and lugged it to the front of the cottage. 'Put it here,' I ordered. He was surprisingly gentle as he laid down the crispy corpse. Softie. I rang the doorbell.

'Shall I get the others out?' Bastion asked; his tone resigned.

'No, I think one dead body makes the point. Though perhaps you should shift.'

The change rolled over him and in an instant he was standing next to me, an alpha predator radiating deadly violence. I patted him on his feathery head. 'Good boy,' I murmured.

He let out an indignant shriek, which made me smile. I was still smiling when the door opened. A female ogre was standing there; like all ogres, one of her limbs was twisted and misshapen. Her left leg was shorter than her right, giving her a limp.

'That must be a pain.' I pointed to the wizened leg. 'Have you tried to have it lengthened a little?' I am not known for my tact.

There was a pause before she responded. 'That would be possible?'

'Not without pain, but yes.'

'Life is pain,' she said dismissively. What an upbeat soul.

'We're returning your people to you.' I gestured at the blackened corpse. 'I'll leave the van open so you can unload the rest.'

'How kind,' she responded drily, no emotion visible.

'I'd like to see High King Krieg.'

'Most would.' She folded her arms.

'I request an audience.'

'Within the den?' She raised her eyebrows and smirked. She thought I was a fool. Luckily, I knew she was wrong.

'By the lake, in the den, or wherever else he wants to meet me.'

'Wait a moment.' She slammed the door in our face.

'They won't let us into the den,' Bastion murmured. It always felt weird to hear his voice come from a beak.

'No,' I agreed, 'but it's always good to give people options and the illusion of choice.'

There was a kraa and a black bird plummeted towards us. I tensed; Krieg's fondness for crows was well known.

'It's Fehu,' Bastion reassured me quickly. Of course it was. Fehu is far bigger than a crow and, as he came closer, his size was obvious. He slowed and settled on my shoulder.

I wasn't quite sure what message we were trying to convey, but it sounded like the start of a bad joke. 'A griffin, a witch and a raven walked into a bar,' I whispered to Bastion. 'It was a crowbar!'

He snorted. 'That's terrible.'

'You only think that because you have no sense of humour.'

Bastion cleared his throat. 'A man comes to a creature bar but the bouncer is a centaur and refuses to let him in. "This bar is for hybrid creatures only," the bouncer says. "For example, my father was a man and my mother was a horse. I just let in a griffin because his father was a lion and his mother was an eagle." The man thinks fast. 'Okay, well then you need to let me in. My father was a Minotaur and my mother was a mermaid."' Bastion stared at me with unblinking golden eyes.

'I don't get it,' I said finally. 'Is it a reference to the feminist text *The Mermaid and the Minotaur* by Dorothy Dinnerstein?'

Bastion huffed. 'No. If you take the human half of the Minotaur and the human half of the mermaid you get a man. That's why the man can get into the bar.'

I waited a beat. 'Are you talking about bars because you're thirsty? I think there's a drink in the van.'

'That joke is hilarious.'

I patted him on his feathered head again. 'Of course it is, Griffin,' I said in my most patronising tone. He glared at me and I struggled to keep my giggles hidden. Who knew that winding up Bastion would be so much fun? It was something to add to my to-do list.

The door swung open. 'You may meet him in the garden. Follow the torches.' The ogre shut the door once more in our faces.

'She seems nice,' I commented facetiously.

'We're not dead yet, so I'll take it,' Bastion murmured. As he led me down the gravel path, I wasn't worried. We were about to enter a negotiation and, like any negotiation, the key was knowing what your opponent wanted.

I knew what Krieg wanted above all else so I had the power here. He just didn't know it yet.

Chapter 21

As we walked, Bastion murmured last-minute instructions to me. 'Refer to the High King as "Your Excellence" at all times. Avoid sustained eye contact. Ensure that you introduce yourself appropriately and bow for at least five seconds. Don't accept any food they offer, and if you have a drink you must hold it with your right hand.'

I sighed. 'And I mustn't let my shadow touch any of the ogres' shadows. I *know*, Bastion.'

'We don't need to worry about their shadows,' he responded gruffly. 'It's dark.'

We followed the gravel path down the side of the cottage, through a gate and into the back garden. It was a huge expanse, complete with a lake that was too large to be called a pond. Bordering the land was a wood. Crows filled the trees, a hundred eager eyes watching our every step. Nothing creepy about that at all.

Krieg sat in the only chair next to a glass table by the side of the lake. The solitary chair was a solid powerplay that I appreciated. There was a log not far from him, but if I sat on it I'd be low on the ground looking up at him and that wouldn't do.

'I'm going to sit on your back,' I murmured to Bastion, trying to keep my lips from moving too much in case Krieg was a lip reader. Bastion grunted, which I took to be an affirmative, though I suppose it could have been exasperation. Grunts are so tricky to translate; I suppose that's why the human language evolved from grunts, clicks and whistles.

Krieg was in his ogre form and, even sitting down, he was huge. There was a reason why he was the king; ogres are terribly impressed by size. They haven't yet worked out that size doesn't matter; it's what you do with it that counts.

He was dressed in leather trousers, a T-shirt and a leather jacket that had to be bespoke to accommodate his overly large right arm. For an ogre, he was pretty good-looking. Ogres are huge, hulking creatures with tusks protruding from their faces. Even with their broad shoulders, their heads are too large for their bodies. They all seem deformed in some way, with misshapen noses or mouths, or one arm longer than the other.

At first glance, Krieg could almost pass as a huge hulking human. He had jet-black hair stylishly tousled in a way that had definitely taken effort to achieve. His jaw was chiselled and clean-shaven; the only thing that marked him as an ogre was his tusks. They protruded from his head, a small one on his forehead and a larger one behind it, a little like a rhinoceros though I doubted he'd love the comparison. It reminded me a little of Rocksteady, the anthropomorphic rhino from *Teenage Mutant Ninja Turtles.* I'd sneered down my nose at the show when I was a teenager, watching it with the other coven kids with open disdain whilst inwardly loving it.

Krieg had another five crows at his feet. He was feeding them scraps and they were cawing with delight. He was doing his best to show that he'd been there the whole while, and that *we* were coming to *him*, but his chest was rising and falling a little too rapidly. He'd run to beat us to the table.

I noted three ogres lingering behind the nearest trees, but I appreciated the fact that no one was openly pointing a crossbow at me. Bastion was incredibly tense and somehow, he seemed even larger than he had been a moment before. Something dangerous was lurking in the air: the promise of violence.

I strolled casually towards Krieg and made a point of looking for another chair. I visibly dismissed the low log that had been none-too-subtly offered as an alternative. 'Griffin,' I said imperiously. 'Come here.'

Because he knew what I had planned, Bastion came over and lowered himself to the ground. I swung my leg over him and my long skirt rose up; it was a good thing I was wearing leggings underneath. When I was safely seated on his back, Bastion stood. Now I was at eye level with the king. And, sitting on him as I was, Bastion and I were in a much better position to make a quick getaway if things got dicey. I am a genius.

'High King Krieg, Your Excellence, it is my honour to meet you this day.' I touched my right hand to my heart and bowed. I held the bow for the count of five then sat up and met Krieg's eyes – just for a second. I saw humour lurking there; he approved of my response to his power play.

Breaking eye contact, I glanced at the cottage. There were ogres' faces at every window. However relaxed Krieg appeared, he was still heavily guarded. Well, so was I. You only needed one Bastion.

'Amber DeLea. I'm surprised to see you here.' Krieg's gaze was curious as he took in Fehu on my shoulder.

'Surprised to see me alive,' I qualified his statement. 'I brought back your compatriots' bodies. I thought that rather than lose even more men in futile combat, you might wish to discuss an alternative. You have a reputation as a clever man.' A little flattery never hurts.

He steepled his fingers. 'I have accepted a contract for the ogres to kill you.'

'I had noticed,' I said drily. 'But I can offer you more than money.' He raised an eyebrow and gestured for me to go on. 'I can help you find your mate.'

He stilled.

Got you.

Chapter 22

Everyone wants to be loved in some capacity. Not everyone wants romantic love, but that was precisely what the rumours said Krieg had been missing from his life. He wasn't asexual yet the space by his side was empty, and culturally for the ogres that was a big deal. If it hadn't already happened, he'd be challenged soon. Every king needed a consort.

Krieg sat back in his seat. He looked relaxed, but he kept his voice low so the ogres hiding in the trees couldn't hear our discussion. 'And how would you do that?' His lips barely moved; maybe I wasn't so far off with my lip-reading paranoia.

'With a potion.'

He studied me again and then gestured to Fehu on my shoulder. 'For all that you have that raven on your shoulder, he does not belong to you. You are a witch without a familiar, which is as absurd as an ogre without a mate. If you cannot find your own familiar with a potion, how would you find my mate?'

Bastion was tense, no doubt worrying about the explosive personal nature of our conversation. 'I once made a potion to find my familiar,' I confessed. 'It told me I already had one. I concluded that I must have bonded with something unknowingly – something unsuited to being a familiar.'

'An ant perhaps,' Krieg sneered.

I didn't rise to his provocation. 'Something of that ilk, yes.' I shrugged like it didn't matter.

'Your potion could be wrong.'

'No, my potions are never wrong. There is nothing I can't brew. Sometimes I can't find the right ingredients, but once I have researched and brewed a potion....' I was lying, of course; I hadn't managed to cure Mum's dementia no matter what mind-sharpening potions I'd invented. I'd tried again and again but she hadn't improved; it was almost like her malady was magical rather than physical.

I was ninety percent telling the truth and ten percent bluffing; fake it till you make it was my strategy here. Besides, I believed with all my heart that I could find his mate ... if he cancelled his contract on me.

'When could you brew this potion?' he asked after a long silence.

I kept my face blank. 'I'm having issues with black witches,' I admitted. 'No doubt that's who hired you.'

'The contract is secured behind a wall of anonymity. I do not know who hired us to kill you.'

'Void the contract and I'll brew you your potion.'

'When?' he asked again with a hint of irritation. Maybe the pressure on him to produce a mate was greater than I'd thought.

'Soon,' I promised, as loosely as I could.

'By the end of April,' he growled.

I shook my head. The end of this month was doable but it didn't leave me much breathing room, not with Abigay's killer on the loose. I had to prioritise that for now. 'It will take me that long to source ingredients,' I lied. 'By the end of May.'

His jaw worked. 'And the black witches?'

'I need to find them and put a stop to them. Permanently.'

He weighed that up. If I was killed, either by an assassin or the black witches, that would end his chance of having a potion made to reveal his mate. He rubbed his bottom lip with his forefinger. 'I know someone who can help you with your witchy problem,' he said finally.

'Who?'

'His name is Voltaire.'

I'd met Voltaire before: he was a vampyr and not just any old vampyr. He was a part of the vampyrs' Red Guard. Their sole purpose is to carry out the vampyrs' black ops, and they travel the world hunting and killing black witches and necromancers. The thought of allying myself with Voltaire made my skin crawl – and yet he was experienced in finding black witches. It wasn't the worst idea. 'Give me his details.'

Krieg studied me. 'No. I'll contact him and tell him about your plight. If he's interested, *he'll* contact you.'

I grimaced. I hate having things out of my control. 'I have a trigger-happy griffin protecting me,' I pointed out. 'Warn him that sliding out of the shadows at the wrong time will get him perma-dead. I've already been attacked by vampyrs seized by necromancy.'

Krieg lifted an eyebrow. 'Have you now? Well then, I can almost guarantee he'll be on the next flight. It was a pleasure meeting you, Miss DeLea. I will pause the contract until the end of May but after that, if you haven't produced my potion, we'll be gunning for you.'

Fantastic. Luckily I work well under pressure.

I recognised a dismissal when I heard one. I nodded like I expected no less and squeezed Bastion with my legs. I had no harness this time but I'd ridden Shirdal without one; as long as Bastion didn't hare off, I'd be fine.

Bastion turned and took a couple of steps before beating his wings and lifting us up and away. It was a brilliant dramatic exit, only foiled by us landing just the other side of the cottage. Bastion shifted back into his human form. I was *not* disappointed that he retained his clothes. We checked the van was empty, slammed the doors closed and drove off.

I opened the windows. The scent of death was lingering in the van and turning my stomach. 'We're alive,' I commented after a few minutes' silence.

'I didn't know you had an ace up your sleeve.'

I flashed him a sudden grin, 'I *always* have an ace up my sleeve.' I grew serious. 'Thank you for letting me ride you, Griffin. That definitely helped change the dynamic.' Bastion's eyes narrowed at me calling him by his species again. Heh, heh, heh; he didn't like it when the shoe was on the other foot.

His eyes flashed gold in the darkness and he sent me a smirk. 'Amber, you can ride me any time,' he purred.

I took my eyes off the road to look at him properly. He was giving me a hot look that I didn't know what to do with. I was pretty confident that he was flirting with me – but surely not? He was just offering me a ride; it was friendly, that was all.

I must be very hard up indeed if I was starting to imagine that *Bastion* was interested in me.

Chapter 23

It was very late when we pulled into the coven's underground car park. Oscar was waiting for us, and he visibly collapsed against his car with relief when he saw me behind the wheel. I felt a pang of guilt; I'd really put him through the mill recently. 'Hey,' I greeted him.

He nodded in return, calm restored, like he hadn't just lifted his head to the ceiling, eyes closed, to thank his God for my safe return.

'I know it's late, but can you come up to my flat?' I asked.

'Sure.' He pushed off the hood of his car. We climbed the stairs in silence and I checked my security at my door. The six on my door was still showing as a nine, so no one had been in my flat. Even shutting the door gently had it swinging down to its rightful place.

Bastion watched me and shook his head. He went to the security box at the side of the door, put in a code and the box beeped once as he deactivated the alarm. I guess his security was a little more effective than mine.

Once inside, I turned on the kettle and took down three mugs. I selected my choices carefully: for Oscar, the words said, *Your secrets are always safe with me. I never even listen when you tell me them*; Bastion's was, *I may love to shop but I will never buy your bull*, and mine said, *Someday you'll go far. I hope you stay there.*

Passive-aggressive mug communication is one of my fortes. I handed out the mugs and Oscar gave me a wry glance. Bastion grinned at his. 'You will,' he said confidently and winked.

I found my lips twitching in return. If nothing else, I had to admire his confidence. I sat and took a sip of my scalding brew. 'So,' I started. 'The other night you two had a conversation about keeping secrets from me. I'd like to hear them.' I hardened my voice and glared. 'Now.'

Bastion and Oscar exchanged a triumphant glance that seemed at odds with what I'd just said.

Oscar cleared his throat and his eyes met mine as he sat forward on the edge of his seat. 'Your mum was fond of oaths and we are both bound tighter than Houdini, but we let you hear as much as we could so that you can start digging. I'm sorry that it hurt, but we can't be open with you. You have to start the conversation. Bastion and I have tried to drop hints numerous times, hoping you'd overhear us.'

I remembered walking into a room a few times and seeing them look up at me weirdly. How many times had they talked loudly about secrets hoping to rouse my curiosity?

'Don't be hard on Oscar,' Bastion interjected. 'This was his plan, his idea. He wants you to know, but we can't tell you outright. We'd die if we did, just like Abigay.' He said it simply but his eyes were intense.

Damn them and damn Mum. Still, some of my sense of hurt and betrayal fizzled away. The trust wasn't completely back – it wouldn't be so easily won a second time – but I felt lighter than I had since I'd heard their conversation. I felt so much better knowing that it was staged, that they'd done it for *my* benefit. Whatever was going on, they were on my side.

I looked at Oscar. 'Abigay told me something on her deathbed – she said that my father was a black witch and that he didn't leave because he had another wife and another life, like I've always believed.'

Oscar looked relieved. 'Thank the Goddess,' he breathed. 'Thank you, Abigay. I guess in the end it didn't matter if your Mum's oath or the witch's curse killed her. Your mum's oaths preclude me from telling you things you don't already know—'

'Like his name?'

'Like that,' he agreed. 'But Abigay was right. Your father was practising black magic. Your mum didn't want you to be raised with that sort of influence around you, but she couldn't condemn the man she'd once loved. Instead of reporting him, she banished him. She told him that if he ever contacted you again, she *would* report him.'

'She has evidence in a safety deposit box?'

He nodded. 'She does.'

'She kept tabs on him?'

'For a while. The other wife, the other life – that did happen but it came later. Then he dropped off the radar.'

'To hide from Mum?'

'Or because he delved even deeper into the black arts,' Oscar suggested grimly.

I thought of Mum's condition and my failure to heal her. My heart thundered as I asked, 'Could her condition be a result of a black curse?'

'No,' he said firmly. 'It's not.'

Something in his tone sent a huge jolt of electricity through me that sent my pulse racing. I set down my mug. 'But you know what the cause is,' I accused him.

He looked at me helplessly, unable to confirm or deny it.

'It's not dementia, is it?' I asked slowly. Oscar didn't answer but his eyes said it all. 'Is there a cure? Can you at least tell me that? Whatever it is, can we undo the damage?'

Suddenly looking all of his sixty-five years, he shook his head. 'No, kid, I don't think so. The damage is done.'

I gritted my teeth. He was wrong; if I knew what was causing the dementia-like symptoms, I could cure her illness. I *could* and I *would*. That was why none of my potions had worked – I'd never made the right one. It wasn't a mind-sharpening potion she needed; it was something else.

Our conversation had been enlightening in some ways and hugely frustrating in others. Now I could tell by the set of his mouth that I wouldn't get any more from him. 'Ria and Meredith?' I asked abruptly, moving to a safer subject.

'Safely with Cain,' he promised. 'They'll stay there until we tell them they can come home.'

I grimaced. 'We'll have to stop Hannah and Edward from helping for now.'

Oscar nodded. 'It doesn't need re-runing for another two weeks. We have time.' Oscar's grandmother was a witch, so Oscar knew more about runes than your average wizard.

Bastion looked between us curiously but didn't ask who Cain was or where Ria and Meredith were. I'd tell him about the circus one day, but not now. There wasn't time.

Time. Time was in short supply. I was being torn in a hundred directions and I felt like I was failing at everything. I needed to find Abigay's killer; I needed to find my father; I needed to work out what was plaguing my mother and heal her; I needed to run my coven and the clinics, and I needed to find Krieg's mate.

My own dream of being the Symposium member for the witches was falling further and further down the list. I told myself that dreams were for children and tried to ignore the bitter sting of disappointment and the deluge of despair that rose up with it.

There were too many things to do. I was going to fail.

Chapter 24

If Oscar and Bastion couldn't tell me what I needed to know, I needed to go directly to the source. I woke early after a restless sleep and felt exhausted the minute my eyes were pried open by the beeping alarm. It shut off abruptly.

'You're still tired,' Bastion murmured. 'Go back to sleep, Amber.'

'I can't.' I kept my eyes closed so he wouldn't see the despair in them. 'There's too much to do and I have too little time. I can create more by getting up early – unless you have access to a hellhound so I can go *back* in time?' I added hopefully.

Hellhounds can create portals to the Third realm enabling a spot of time travel. I'd have given a lot to go back in time to speak to my mum while she still had full control of her faculties. Heck, if I could go back in time I could go back and meet my father and demand his name and location.

'I don't – and even if I did I wouldn't recommend it. Without a permanent bond with the hellhound to protect your mind, too much time in the Third realm scrambles your brains.'

I thought of Leo Harfen – an elf who had spent too much time in the Third – and nodded. 'I know.' I sighed. That is the reason the Symposium controls the main portal to the Third realm and strictly monitors who can go through it. Housed in St Luke's in Liverpool, known colloquially as 'the bombed-out church', it is guarded by black-ops wizards who are ready to kill to prevent unauthorised incursions. Time is not to be meddled with lightly; it is *supposed* to be linear.

I pried my eyes open again and forced myself to get up. I texted Oscar, asking if he wanted to go to see Mum, then I went into the bathroom with fresh clothes slung over my arm, hoping a hot shower would rejuvenate me.

I dried and runed myself for the day and slid on clean clothes. I looked into my bathroom mirror and said my affirmations but I couldn't decide on a goal for the day; there were just too many. Because I knew I needed it, I went into my room and pulled out my gratitude journal.

I am grateful for... I hesitated. I didn't feel grateful to-day, I felt weary and beaten. Not a good mindset to start the morning.

I am grateful to have freed Benji from the underground for however long it lasts. I am grateful my mum is alive. I am grateful for having Oscar in my life. I am grateful for the orange juice in my fridge. I hesitated and then added the fifth thought; it was the one that had crossed my mind the first moment I'd opened the journal but I'd denied it. I needed to be honest with myself if no one else, so I wrote it down. *I am grateful for Bastion.* There it sat in black and white.

Unbelievable as it was, it was true. I was grateful for his solid, taciturn presence in my life; I was grateful for the kindness he showed in giving me books and saving my life over and over again. I was grateful for his companionship; he was refreshingly non-judgemental and I never felt that he was giving me marks out of ten. He was just *there.* Today, because I was tired and my barriers were lowered, I could admit to myself that I was dreading the end of his contract with me.

I put the journal back in my bedside drawer and pulled out my athame. It is a family heirloom and it has all manner of protections etched into the pommel. I wasn't going to be defenceless – like Bastion, I learned from my mistakes. I sheathed it in an ankle holster hidden by my long swishy skirt.

Bastion strode in from his shower wearing black boxers but nothing else, bar the water droplets that clung to his tanned skin. Which I definitely didn't notice.

I was about to avert my gaze, when I noticed a rune on his inner thigh, so small that I had never noticed it before. My eyes narrowed. His boxers were rolled up a little – deliberately – so that the rune was visible rather than covered. He was deliberately showing it to me. 'What is that?' I breathed.

He stood stock-still, gave me an approving look but said nothing. I was certain now that this was the reason Bastion kept prancing around all-but nude. I slid off the bed, fell to my knees and pressed my face close to his groin so I could study his inner thigh.

I stroked the lines of the rune and frowned darkly. It was a supressing rune, *perthro,* the symbol for the unknown and secrets. I recognised the elaborate style right away: it was one of Mum's.

The whorls and embellishments she'd used told me she had meant this *perthro* to suppress – but what? And it was no simple rune, it was a tattoo, which meant that

Mum used her magic every single day to keep it active. It would continue to work, no matter the distance, though the drain on her magic must be huge. No wonder she had to recharge as regularly as she did.

It was a suppressing rune but what was it suppressing? The urge to kill, perhaps? I'd never heard of such a thing succeeding. I looked up at him, 'Why is my mum protecting you so much?' I asked desperately.

'Because she knew I'd protect you.'

'Why?'

A moment of tension hummed between us, then: 'Amber? Bastion?' Oscar called, his voice muffled by the front door. 'Can one of you let me in? I don't know the code.'

'You'd best get it,' Bastion said huskily. 'I need a minute.'

I started to ask why but then my eyes dropped and I froze as I suddenly realised what a compromising position we were in. I was kneeling in front of him, my breath ghosting along his inner thighs, and his body had visibly reacted to having me – anyone, I'm sure – so close to ground zero.

My eyes widened as I took in the size of him. I involuntarily licked my lips, before scrambling to my feet, cheeks flaming. 'I'll come!' I called to Oscar.

COVEN OF THE WITCH

'You would,' Bastion murmured in a low promise that made me tingle in interesting places. He *was* flirting with me. There was no way to deny it now. Bastion was attracted to me. And I didn't have the first clue what to do about it.

175

Chapter 25

Mum looked at me blankly and it hurt so much that I struggled to hold back tears. I motioned Oscar forward, and stepped back to stand at the window. All I wanted was to talk to her. Was that so much to ask? My heart ached; she was here with me but I couldn't get the maternal support I so desperately needed, not to mention the answer to the hundred questions whirling in my brain.

As I tried not to cry, I gazed out at the grounds around the care home. A griffin stepped out from her hiding place behind a huge oak tree, and I had a moment of panic before I recognised her. It was Charlize, Bastion's daughter, and she was here to guard my mum, not kill her.

Charlize gave me a cheeky salute before disappearing from sight again. I'd saved her from a black witch so we had a reasonable relationship, which I was pleased about though I didn't want to examine why. It was a relief to know she was here, guarding Mum.

One tiny slice of tension dropped away. I should have asked Bastion earlier what measures he'd taken to keep Mum safe. He'd called in the big guns: his flesh and blood was guarding my flesh and blood. We were enmeshed in so many ways.

'Luna.' Oscar greeted my mum warmly. 'You look beautiful.' I heard the love in his voice and it threatened to undo me completely.

'As do you,' she replied lightly. 'I love this little goatee you've grown.'

They talked quietly and Mum told him about a landscape painting she'd made the previous day. Her room was littered with paintings; now that they wouldn't let her paint runes, she'd embraced art and she wasn't half bad. I busied myself looking through her work, keeping half an ear on her conversation with Oscar.

When he cleared his throat and told her he had some bad news, I turned back to them. 'I'm sorry, Luna,' he said. 'Abigay is dead.'

I expected grief to wash over Mum but instead fury reigned supreme. I guess that told me where I got my reactions from. 'How?' she spat.

'Murdered. By a black witch.'

Mum gave an unladylike snarl and Lucille chittered at her, running up her body to wind around her neck and comfort her. Mum acknowledged her with a gentle pat then she looked at me, her gaze sharp. 'Find her killer, Amber,' she ordered. 'To murder the Crone? The black coven grows far too bold.'

'You know about the black coven?' I gaped.

'Of course I do! Why do you think I told you so many stories about them?'

'But they were *stories*. I never thought they were real.'

'Well, now you know, child.'

'My father... What is his name?'

Her face grew hard. 'You leave him alone, Amber. Do you hear me?'

'And what if he's involved in this? Do you expect me to look the other way because we share some blood?' I demanded.

She shifted on her seat and blew out a long breath. 'He is *dangerous,* Amber, perhaps even to you.'

'I don't care. I need to know his name.'

She waved my demand aside. 'It won't help you. He will have changed it by now – he'll have a new name and, if he's sensible, a new face. You can do a great deal with plastic surgery and healing runes. I doubt I would recognise him these days if he strolled past me. He always had contingency plans and he loved to consider every possibility. It drove me wild, actually.'

'Mum, please.' My voice broke as I gave in to the urge I'd been fighting since I had come in, and I flew towards her for a hug.

She stood as I came closer, reading my intention, and let me into her arms. 'The world is on your shoulders and I'm so sorry for that.' She held me tightly and kissed my cheek. 'I love you so much, Amber.'

I squeezed her back, so grateful for this moment with her that I felt like my heart would burst.

'Shaun,' she murmured into my hair with a sigh. 'His name was Shaun. You'll find out more in my safety deposit box in Liverpool.' She drew back from me and kissed my forehead one last time, then opened the dresser drawer, pulled out a little box and lifted out a small metal key. She held it out to me. It had 989 written on it.

'And Bastion? Why have you runed him?' I asked.

She looked at me ruefully. 'Leave me some secrets, Amber. They're all I've got.'

'If you keep them for too long, you'll forget them. Please, Mum,' I pleaded desperately.

'Not today, Amber,' she said firmly in the hard, unwavering voice that she'd used to chastise me when I was a teenager. 'That one will unravel in the right time and place.' She put her hands on her hips, 'You still haven't sought out the prophecy, have you?'

I shook my head. 'I don't—'

'—believe in prophecy,' she finished for me. 'I know, Amber.' She grimaced. 'With hindsight, I shouldn't have pish-poshed prophecy quite so much when you were growing up, but I didn't want you to set much store by it. I didn't want you hunting for yours until you were ready. But if Abigay is dead, the time is nigh.' She looked at me solemnly. 'You're strong enough for this.'

'I don't feel strong,' I admitted in a small voice. 'Not today.'

'You are the strongest woman I know,' she said confidently. 'I made sure of it. But we all have off days and that's okay too.'

I didn't know how much I needed her reassurance until she gave it to me. Even for someone over forty, there was nothing like having your mother kiss your boo-boo and tell you it would be okay. That *you* were okay.

Steel returned to my spine. She was right: I *was* a strong woman and now I was going to prove it to my enemies.

Chapter 26

Mum lost her lucidity soon after that. She smiled cautiously at Oscar and me. 'Do I know you?' she asked us both lightly.

Oscar smiled gently. 'Not today. But thank you for your fine company.' He set his teacup down. 'I do love this landscape you've painted.' He pointed to one on the pile. 'May I buy it from you?'

'Oh,' she clapped her hands, delighted. 'Honestly, it's just a pleasure to *create*. To know that someone is enjoying my work would bring me such great joy. I've always painted.' She frowned. 'At least, I think I have.'

Her expression cleared. 'I don't need money. You take whichever one you like.' She turned to me. 'You can take one too. It'll give me room to paint more.' She gave me a cheeky wink that was so reminiscent of the woman I had known who was still in there, somewhere.

'Sure,' I agreed easily. 'Thank you very much, Ms De-Lea.'

'Please, call me Luna.'

I'd rather call you Mum, I thought, but I said nothing. I thumbed through the artwork and selected a painting that had already called to me, a confusion of numbers and letters swirling around a staircase. It looked how I felt – muddled and disjointed. 'I'd like this one, if I may,' I said impulsively.

'Of course – but are you sure?' She frowned dubiously. 'That's not my best work. This landscape is much prettier. I know! Here, you can take both.'

'If you're certain.' I accepted both the paintings.

I gave Lucille a farewell pat and she chittered happily at me. 'How strange,' Mum remarked. 'She's not often friendly to strangers.' She frowned again.

'I've always been an animal person,' I lied. I didn't want her to get distressed.

Oscar and I said our goodbyes and let ourselves out. Bastion raised his eyebrows as we emerged laden with canvasses. 'She's been painting,' I explained. I cleared my throat. 'Thanks – for Charlize.'

'You're welcome. Shirdal has been taking the night shift, so Luna is guarded around the clock.'

'Thank you,' Oscar echoed my words. 'That makes me feel better.'

'And me,' I added.

Bastion blinked. 'I should have mentioned it earlier. I'm not used to thinking of others.'

I thought of the books he'd given me and gave him a little jostle with my shoulder, 'You're doing okay.' He smiled, and my tummy felt like it was full of butterflies.

Oh heck. I fancied Bastion.

I tried to keep the realisation off my face. It didn't matter that I thought he was kind and reliable and sexy as hell, he was my bodyguard and getting involved with your bodyguard never ends well. Anyway, I *couldn't* get involved because, attraction or not, Jake's spectre lingered between us, glaring at me with accusing eyes. It was wrong.

Wrong, I told myself firmly. I was going to put this ... feeling ... for Bastion into a little box and forget all about it. I was entirely too busy to think of doing anything about my raging hormones, and anyway, wasn't I supposed to be going through the menopause right about now? Instead, I was feeling distinctly teenaged. Life was ridiculous.

'Where to?' Oscar asked.

'The coven first,' I said firmly. 'I need to spend some time in my office, then we'll head to Liverpool and see if we

HEATHER G. HARRIS

can get into this safety deposit box. Do you know which bank she was with?'

'If it's in Liverpool,' Bastion interjected, 'it'll be Liverpool Vaults, the only private bank in the city. The high street banks offer far fewer safety deposit box services these days.'

'Where is Liverpool Vaults?' I asked.

'It's in the Royal Liver Building. It won't be easy to get in. There are biometric tests as well as a code – and, of course, the key.'

Of course it wouldn't be easy. My eyebrows rose. 'Mum loves that building,' I commented. On top of it are two huge statues of the Liver Birds that rear up onto the skyline, fifteen feet tall and made of copper. The story goes that Bella and Bertie protect the city; I'd even heard it said that was why the Connection made its headquarters in Liverpool rather than London or Manchester. The protection of the two Liver Birds was nothing to be sniffed at.

The legend says that the female looks out to sea, watching for sailors to return safely home, while the male looks into the city and watches over the seafarers' families – and makes sure the pubs are open, as the Scousers often joke. Legend also dictates that the birds face away from each other: if they were to mate and fly away, the city would

COVEN OF THE WITCH

cease to exist. The statues are chained to the Liver Building because if they were to leave Liverpool, the River Mersey would burst its banks and flood it.

Despite travelling to Liverpool with Mum and visiting the city alone numerous times since, I'd never seen the real Liver Birds. They become visible only when they want to, and only when the city is under threat. But one thing was for sure, Bertie and Bella *had* mated. They had a plethora of children that could also be spotted around the city, and the city had never fallen. So that part of the legend mustn't be true.

Bastion was right. Mum loved the legends of the Liver Birds so no doubt she would have entrusted her valuables to a company housed in the Liver Building. Now there was just the small matter of getting through the biometric tests to access her possessions. Easy-peasy.

Chapter 27

Before we went off for a spot of breaking and entering, I returned to the coven. Ethan, Jacob and Jeb had been running things smoothly between them. The roster for the next two weeks was already done, and Jacob had taken over my teaching duties. Ethan had started brewing additional warding and healing potions because he'd noted the stores were getting low. In fact, Briony Fields had been the one to notify him of the diminished stores as he hadn't had time to do a stock check yet this week.

Everything about his report made me feel proud; the coven were really pulling together now that the threat of a black witch wasn't hanging over them. Little white lies *do* have a time and place. That there were no black witches in our coven felt more like a grey lie than a white one, but my intention was good and that's what counted.

There was a knock on my door. 'Come in!' I called.

Hannah entered followed by Edward, who stood by the door and quickly scanned the room. I gave him a small nod of approval; Hannah was one of the coven's rising stars and I was grateful to see her being guarded properly.

'Sit,' I gestured for her to take my spare chair, which was runed lightly with truth runes.

She sat. 'It's good to see you, Coven Mother.'

'And you, Hannah. How can I help?'

She settled her hands deliberately in her lap in an effort to stop fidgeting and took a deep breath. 'Have I done something wrong, Coven Mother?'

'Wrong?'

'I was told my assistance was no longer required with the circus.'

'Ah. For now – but it's a temporary measure. You will be there again soon, no doubt.'

'Oh.' She shot me a relieved smile. 'I thought I had let you down somehow.'

'Not at all. Your work is exemplary, as always, but your skills can be better deployed at this time,' I lied smoothly.

'Of course.' Hannah stood. 'I won't take up anymore of your time. Good day, Coven Mother.'

Edward opened the door for her and checked the corridor. It seemed that even within the tower he was taking her wellbeing very seriously.

Hannah hesitated before leaving. 'I'm sorry about the Crone.'

I nodded, smiling tightly, keeping a firm grip on my emotions. She and Edward stepped out and the door shut behind them.

'She didn't believe you about the reason she's been pulled off the job,' Bastion noted.

'No, probably not, but it can't be helped.' I shrugged. Hannah probably suspected that someone had now joined the circus that I didn't want her to know about. Unfortunately, that was bang on the money.

No one else darkened my door as I tapped away at my laptop for another twenty minutes. After I was satisfied that my coven wasn't disintegrating without me, Bastion and I headed to the potion store whilst Oscar packed our bags for a few nights away.

Sarah Bellington was on shift, standing diligently and alertly at the desk. 'Coven Mother!' she greeted me enthusiastically. 'You're back!'

'Not for long,' I said with genuine regret.

COVEN OF THE WITCH

Sarah's face became serious. 'I heard about the Crone – we all did. We're so sorry. I know you were close.'

A rock took residence in my throat. I don't know why but I hadn't been prepared for her sympathy; I'd expected Sarah to be pissed off about her demotion, not to look at me with such empathy. It blindsided me more than Hannah's sympathy had. 'Thank you,' I managed.

'Jeb has been going over safety rules with me,' she said brightly. 'He's the best.' She sighed dreamily, leaned on the desk and cupped her face with one hand. Uh-oh: someone had a crush. Jeb was quite attractive, but he was in his late thirties and she was barely an adult so I didn't rate her chances.

'He is,' I agreed, and left it at that. 'I need privacy in the stores for a moment. Please don't let anyone else in.'

She straightened. 'Of course not! You can count on me!'

Experience told me otherwise but we all deserve a second chance – or, in her case, a third one. I patted her shoulder and went into the depths of the store. At the very back of it was a chilled safe that only Ethan, Jeb and I had access to.

Bastion followed me in, politely turning his back while I tapped the code to open it. The heavy door swung open and I reached for the top shelf. I took one potion and then, after a moment's hesitation, I took a second.

Potion bombs are expensive to produce or buy. Each witch carries one on his or her person at all times. They act as both a threat and a deterrent; they help prevent anyone attacking us because they think witches are an easy target – with our potion bombs, we're not.

We don't have immortality like the dragons, super speed like the vampyrs, deadly claws like the griffins or the IR like the wizards, so we should be low on the power rung but we're not. We work hard to be invaluable to other species; we curry favours and make allies like other species breathe. We need to in order to survive. And if all that fails, we have our bombs.

When a witch dies, their potion bomb is passed back to their coven for redistribution. I'd used mine and Abigay's in the last few days. The ones in the safe replace any that have been used. I'd need to fill in an incident form to report mine as used, but I simply didn't have time for bureaucracy right now. Taking a second potion bomb is strictly prohibited, but I was hunting black witches and they knew it. Only a fool wouldn't double up on weapons in those circumstances. And I am no fool.

I noted my use of my potion bomb in the log and also documented the use of Abigay's, though I didn't specify who had used it. I recorded that two replacement bombs had been allocated, but again didn't specify to whom. I was fudging the paperwork but it was better than nothing.

As I hustled out of the store, I encountered Melrose. 'Where are they?' she demanded loudly. 'Where are Merry and Ria?'

Damn it. 'They are taking a short break. Losing Cindy has been hard on Meredith.'

'Exactly! She should have her friends – her coven – around her.' Melrose stamped her foot. 'Coven Mother, I'm concerned. If they're just taking a holiday, why aren't they answering their phones? This isn't normal.'

'They're taking an unplugged break,' I lied smoothly. 'No tech, no TV, back to nature.'

The certainty that something was wrong faded from Melrose's eyes but she was still glaring at me suspiciously. 'If they're not back in a week, I'll know something is going on.'

I watched her stalk off, wondering if she was merely concerned or if she was the black witch in my coven trying to find her acolyte. It was hard to look at everyone with suspicion, and I wasn't enjoying it one bit. Normally I *knew* who not to trust, but now the slate had been wiped clean and the only ones I believed in were Oscar and Bastion. It was a depressingly short list.

Frustratingly, I didn't have time to focus on finding the witch who had turned Ria and planted a bomb in my bedroom because now I had to find Abigay's killer instead. Task prioritisation is one of my super powers. I am brilliant at organisation, as good as Abigay herself, and her mind had been like a steel trap. I had seen no evidence that she had needed notes or aide-mémoires, even at the end. I hoped I was as sharp as her when I was in my eighties. If I lived to be eighty.

Chapter 28

The drive to Liverpool was soothing. Oscar's solid presence at the wheel was usually enough to relax me but, seeing how tense I was, he put on some relaxing classical music. I let the symphonies wash over me in all their beauty; maybe in another life I had played a musical instrument.

When I was growing up, Mum hadn't allowed time for such frivolities; it was rune work, potion work, ingredient properties and interactions. Rinse and repeat. And, of course, I'd had a normal education in a state school too because it wouldn't do to not have a basic education as well as a witchy one.

I loved the thought of Emory's Other Academy, a school where magical kids could go and learn both without having to hide their Otherness from their school friends. It had been hard growing up; when other kids talked about TV shows, I'd had nothing to contribute because what might have been TV time had been taken up with runic studies.

Bastion sat next to me in the middle seat, not one seat over. Easier to throw his wings around me if necessary, I supposed. The warmth of his thigh against mine was incredibly distracting and my fingers itched to reach out and touch him through the thin fabric of his cargo trousers. I'd be able to feel the hard corded muscles of his powerful thigh through those trousers... My stomach felt hot and fluttery at the thought. He was so close.

I looked at him more than once during the journey and his gaze was always on me. Each time, I looked away and stared fixedly through the window. Tension was building between us that I didn't have the first clue what to do with except deny it. But as time moved on, I was finding it harder and harder to do that. I didn't *want* to deny it. My life was precarious and I'd been alone for a long time; it was more than twenty years since I'd shared more than a kiss on the cheek. Twenty years. I'd all but forgotten what a real kiss felt like.

To distract myself, I sent Benji a quick text to check in with him. He sent back a smiley face and thumbs up; he'd been thrilled when I'd shown him emojis.

We drew up to Liverpool's coven tower. As a matter of courtesy I'd already sent a text to Kassandra to let her know I was coming, plus I needed her help. I wasn't certain she wasn't a black witch but she'd helped Jinx a time or two, and one of those times had involved rooting out daemon influence. I was sure a black witch would have let that chaos run amok. I was eighty percent sure that I could trust her, and at a time like this, eighty percent would have to do.

We parked in the coven car park and made our way upstairs, Oscar walking two steps ahead of me, Bastion two steps behind. I felt a bit like a movie star; I only needed some morally deficient paparazzi to invade my privacy and I'd be all set.

Bernard was on the concierge desk and he beamed when he saw me. 'Coven Mother! How lovely to see you.' He lowered his voice and lost the smile. 'Terrible business, losing the Crone like that. Terrible.'

Phrases like that piss me off. 'Losing the Crone' made it seem like she was a toy that we'd accidentally misplaced instead of a woman who had been brutally murdered. 'Indeed,' was my clipped response. 'Is Kassandra available now?' She'd better be.

'Of course, Coven Mother. She's expecting you. Go on up to her office.'

We took the stairs, more because Bastion said that the main lifts were a security risk than because I wanted the exercise. Oscar had his lighter in his hand ready to flambé anyone who attacked me. He was on high alert – but so were we all. Being braced for an attack 24/7 was tiring and I wasn't sure how long we could go on living like this. The tension was certainly killing me.

I knocked firmly on the door. 'Come,' Kassandra's voice rang from inside.

We entered and my eyebrows shot up. Kassandra wasn't alone: there were two women with her whom I didn't recognise. One had short blonde hair with one side shaved; her arms were covered in tattoos, though none of them were runes as far as I could see. The other woman was a pretty green-eyed brunette; what made my lips press into a line was the uniform she was wearing. A quick glance to her shoulders confirmed it: she was an inspector from the Connection.

She stood, touched her hand to her heart and gave a little bow. 'My honour to meet you, Miss DeLea. I have heard a great deal about you.'

'Only good things, I hope,' I responded tightly, bowing in response. I raised an eyebrow at Kassandra in a clear *what the heck?*

'This is Inspector Stacy Wise – she works with Elvira,' Kassandra explained. 'She's here to discuss the Crone's murder.'

I glared at them both. 'That is an internal matter and at this stage there is no suggestion that another species is involved. As such, it falls under the edict of an internal conflict and will be resolved by the covens and their ruling body.'

Stacy's smile was even and professional. 'I'm not here to interfere. Kassandra and I were merely comparing notes. I work out of Chester. There have been a number of ... incidents.'

'What sort of incidents?'

'Whether I tell you depends on whether we're sharing information or not,' she replied coolly.

'I share information with Elvira,' I said stubbornly, crossing my arms. 'I'll speak to her.'

'Elvira's not available. She's in the field. I can help you.'

'I don't know you.'

'And if you don't talk to me, you never will.' It was a fair point delivered in a sharp tone. I was starting to like this Stacy Wise.

'How do I know that you are competent?' I asked, deliberately trying to rile her.

'Because I am,' she assured me calmly, not rising to the bait.

'No one who is incompetent recognises that they're incompetent,' I argued.

'You're wrong. A number of my colleagues are fully aware they're not worth the air they breathe.'

'That's the problem with Daddy securing their role,' I muttered. I hate incompetence.

'Indeed.'

'Do you have a rich daddy?'

'I do not,' she confirmed, a ghost of a smile darting across her face.

I felt myself smile involuntarily. I *was* starting to like her. 'And who is this?' I gestured to the other woman.

'Oh!' Kassandra blinked, 'Sorry, I didn't realise you hadn't met. This is Stevie, my second in command.'

Stevie bowed to me, 'My honour to meet you, Coven Mother.' Her tone was sufficiently respectful to mollify me.

I gave her a little bob of my head. 'My honour to meet you, Stevie. And what is this?' I asked, gesturing to the three of them. 'Hubble, bubble, toil and trouble?'

'An unholy triune,' Kassandra admitted with a wink. 'The three of us have been friends for a long while. Stacy was just discussing the latest goings-on in Chester.'

'Do tell,' I said blandly.

Stacy eyed me warily. 'There have been two separate incidents. We've passed them off in the media as grave robberies.'

'But they're not?'

'No, we don't believe so. The bodies were both magical in nature.'

'How so?'

'One was a deceased griffin and one was a deceased wizard.' Behind me, I felt Bastion tense.

'You suspect necromancy,' I said flatly.

'I do.'

'So you've come to your local coven.'

'Not to accuse them,' Stacy said firmly, 'but to put them on guard. Someone is practising black magic and I think that they're smart enough not to do it in their own back yard. Chester is a little further afield.'

'Not by much.'

'No, but by enough.'

I didn't argue the point. 'Have you spoken to the Red Guard?' I asked.

'No, but they are aware of the robberies.'

'How?'

'I don't know who tipped them off, but they were at the scene before we were.' She grimaced; obviously she hadn't been pleased by their presence. At least we were on the same page about that.

'You don't think it's possible that vampyrs were stealing corpses?' I thought it unlikely but I wanted to test her response.

'I considered it, but no. They need something living to eat from, so they have no interest in the dead flesh.' She grinned suddenly. 'Besides, Voltaire was hopping mad. I don't think he's a good enough actor to pull the wool over my eyes.'

Voltaire again. That prick just kept coming up like an irritating, perpetual erection. It was horrifying that Dick Symes' pecker was the first thing that came to mind on the heels of that thought. Eww. I dragged my mind away from him and focused on the Red Guard vampyr. I'd have to speak to Voltaire, but not now. Now I had other things to do.

I sighed and looked at Kassandra and Stevie. 'Keep your investigations quieter than quiet. The Crone was travelling up and down the country hunting out black witches. It's no coincidence that she was killed before she could present her findings. The black witches are clearing up their mess so you don't want them knowing you're digging around.'

'Them, plural?' Stevie asked, her voice sharp.

I nodded slowly. 'Plural,' I agreed grimly.

Kassandra swore and her lizard familiar, Jax, let out a little chitter to reassure her. Then she gave a little gasp, grimaced and touched her hand to her lower back. My eyes narrowed – she was in pain. Jax made a sad noise, glowed a little and relief washed over Kassandra's face as the pain ebbed with his assistance. She stroked his head and he swung down to nestle into her chest. I suppressed a shudder. I *hate* reptiles. I'd already spotted Stevie's snake, coiled around her arm blending marvellously with her tattoo sleeve. I'd be giving her wide berth.

I looked pointedly at Inspector Wise. 'That was information sharing, but it's all I'll give you for now. This is an internal matter. Keep yourself safe. And out of it.' My voice was a shade off a threat.

Stacy smiled. 'I'm an inspector, I'm never safe.' She pushed off the wall she was leaning against. 'I'll be seeing you,' she promised. As she walked past Bastion, she greeted him quietly. 'Bastion.'

'Wise,' he murmured. She shut the door behind her.

'I need help,' I said baldly to Kassandra. 'And the fewer people who know about it, the better.'

Stevie stood. 'That's my cue to leave, I suppose.' She bowed again to me, 'If you do need me, Coven Mother, I'm always happy to help. Kassandra has spoken very highly of you. A friend of hers is a friend of mine.' She left and I breathed a little easier with one less reptile to freak out over.

Kassandra smiled warmly at me. 'How can I help you?'

I sighed then told her.

Chapter 29

There are some things a witch can't do to herself and one of them is making illusion runes. When you paint illusion runes on someone or something to make them appear differently, you need someone to act as a focus and someone to act as the depositor. The focus has to imagine what the illusion will be, down to the last toenail and flyaway hair. You cannot possibly hold that focus and paint runes at the same time; nor, as the depositor, can you do anything other than lie still and have runes painted on you.

Oscar had his eyes closed, imagining my mum in his mind with all of his strength, whilst I lay on Kassandra's desk. I was wearing nothing but my blue lacy underwear, giving Kassandra swathes of pale, almost translucent skin to work with. I don't get much sun. I tried not to feel hideously self-conscious that Bastion was seeing me in matching underwear for the first time sprawled across

Kassandra's desk. It wasn't supposed to be like that. Not that I'd thought about it. At all. Ever.

When I risked a glance in his direction, he was studiously looking away from me. Was it because I repulsed him? Or because *he* didn't want to see me virtually naked for the first time like this? I was wrong-footed and I hated it. At any one time, I always knew what I was doing and why, but with Bastion I didn't know what the heck was going on.

I pushed thoughts of him aside and focused. I already looked a lot like my mum – her genes had bred true – but not enough to pass through the biometric security of the vault. That meant that everything had to be perfect; there could be no doubt that I was who I said I was.

After innumerable runes had been painted on my skin with cold, slimy potions, it was Oscar's turn. Kassandra painted a rune onto his forehead and cheeks, moments later the magic in the runes was activated. The activation meant that the runes were dry enough for me to dress so I pulled on my usual black skirt and peasant blouse. I'd inherited my style from my mother so no one would look at me – her – twice.

Oscar was looking at me weirdly and I gave him a sympathetic glance. It must have been hard for him to see me wearing my mum's face.

'You've got an hour,' Kassandra warned. 'Two at most.'

'Thank you.'

'What are friends for?'

I blinked. 'We're not friends. We're friendly rivals at best.'

'No, we're definitely friends,' Kassandra said firmly, smiling at me.

'Are you sure?' I asked dubiously.

'Quite. Go on now, Amber. The clock is ticking.'

I felt unsettled. There were a number of truths that I had used to define myself over the years: one, I was a witch; two, I was a *good* witch; three, I didn't have a familiar; four, I didn't have friends. Yet now I had Jinx, Lucy, and Benji – and I certainly had something friendly with Bastion. Now this. Apparently Kassandra was my friend and I didn't know quite what to do with her.

'Will you ring me one time?' I asked quietly. 'Just to chat?'

Kassandra looked momentarily bowled over before she stood and closed the distance between us. She hugged me.

'I absolutely will,' she promised, her voice full of emotion. 'And Amber?'

'Yes?'

'My friends call me Kass.'

I smiled. Kass; I could do that. If Kass did turn out to be a black witch, it would hurt like a bitch. Not for the first time, I wished Jinx were not on holiday. 'If we're friends, shouldn't you tell me about your condition?' I asked. Maybe I could help.

She sighed and sent me a rueful look. 'I have fibromyalgia. We can talk about my fibro another time. The clock is ticking.'

'There are potions for fibro, aren't there?'

Kass shook her head. 'Nothing specifically for it. It's a bit like Common treatment –something for the pain, something for the depression, but no cure. It's all about management.'

'That sucks.'

She grinned. 'Yeah, it does. But you know what? It does feel a little better to share about it. A problem shared is a problem halved. Now go! Scoot!'

'Yes ma'am,' I quipped.

'I have a private lift.' Kass stepped back and pulled on a book on her shelf, revealing a metal door. She pressed a button and the door dinged open. 'This will take you straight to the car park so there'll be fewer eyes on your disguise.'

I raised an eyebrow at Bastion. He nodded, looking resigned. 'Thank you,' I said to the other Coven Mother.

'You're welcome, Amber.' Kass hugged me again and I reciprocated carefully. I wasn't familiar enough with her condition to know if a hug would hurt her, but I'd find out. I added 'learn about fibro' to my to-do list.

The three of us stepped into the private lift and I gave Kass an awkward wave as the doors slid closed. Apparently Bastion's objection to lifts had been overruled by our need to be quick and unseen.

We hummed down to the underground and into the waiting car. We weren't far from the Liver Building so it didn't take long to navigate the one-way system to park behind it. The drive had been weird because Bastion sat on the other side of the car from me. Was he really repulsed by me?

'You'd best stay here,' I said as briskly as I could.

He shook his head. 'I'll walk you to the building and keep watch out. Oscar can go into the building with you, though he won't be allowed to enter the vault. Have you got a potion bomb with you?'

I nodded. 'And my athame.'

He nodded. His face was blank, but his body belied the impassivity of his expression: he was tense. Nervous about being apart from me, perhaps? I felt the same; I felt vulnerable, with an itch between my shoulder blades that I couldn't scratch. 'Let's move.'

True to his word, Bastion set up position to loiter outside.

Oscar walked in with me. The Liver Building held a number of businesses, which was good because it gave us a viable reason to stroll into it. We took the stairs to the right floor. The reception area was swanky, decked out with thick carpet, plush chairs and modern dangling lights. There were no windows that I could see: complete privacy from start to finish.

I smiled confidently at the receptionist. 'Hello, I'd like to make a withdrawal.'

'Of course. Your name, please?'

'Luna DeLea.'

'Date of birth?'

I rattled it off.

'Vault number?'

'Nine-eight-nine.'

She tapped away at the computer and then frowned. I stepped in closer. In the reflection of the mirror behind her, I saw the numbers on her screen were inverted. I was holding the key the wrong way up. 'Oh! Sorry! Six-eight-six.' I laughed lightly. 'What am I like?'

Her expression cleared. 'No problem.' She tapped again and then pressed a buzzer. Almost immediately a man in a smart pinstripe suit came out to meet me. I waited for him to arrest me but instead he gave me a cool, professional smile. 'If you would follow me, Miss DeLea, your companion can wait here.' He gestured to the purple seats.

Oscar sank grudgingly into one of the chairs in the waiting room whilst I trailed behind the suited-and-booted man down a long narrow corridor. I was anxious; fingering the potion bottle in my pocket as I tried not to think what a good place this would be to ambush me.

At the end of the corridor there was a security panel. 'An eye scan, if you please, ma'am.'

Crap. I leaned forward, preparing all of my excuses for when it failed – but it didn't fail. The light flashed green and the man smiled at me and led me in.

Thank goodness. Oscar must have spent decades gazing into my mum's eyes with enough attention to replicate them. Actually, it was a bit creepy.

I struggled not to gape when we entered the vault. Gold security lockers lined the walls; the room looked incredibly opulent, and I could only imagine the depth of the riches it contained. We walked to box 686 and I fished out my key. The man pulled out his matching key and we inserted them at the same time.

The front of the locker swung open, and he removed the box. 'I'll take you to a private room where you can open the box and peruse it at your leisure. Follow me.'

We went into a side room, which he opened with a six-digit code. I wasn't sure what I'd been expecting, but it wasn't this decadent space with art on the walls and a chaise-longue. He put the box down on a mahogany table and left me to it.

I wasted no time; illusion spells are temperamental at best, so we were up against the clock. I opened my tote bag and set it next to the box, then lifted the box lid. I grimaced at my trembling hands. Now was not the time to get nervous. Just because I was breaking the law, it was no reason to be feeble, I told myself firmly, though with no visible effect. My hands still shook.

All the box held was a thick brown envelope, which I stuffed into my tote. I *really* wanted to open it, but now wasn't the time or place because I had to hustle. I shouldered my bag, shut the box and opened the door.

If the man was surprised at the speed of my visit, he didn't show it. He took the box and I shoved my hands into my pockets so he wouldn't see them trembling. We went back into the vault, placed the box back in its locker and swung the door shut. It locked with a clunk. The man tested it was closed by tugging on it, but it didn't shift.

'If you'll follow me,' he murmured, and led me back to the waiting room where a tense Oscar was still sitting.

'All done,' I chirped reassuringly. 'Let's go.'

Oscar rose and we walked out as calmly as possibly. I waved goodbye to the receptionist. My mum had been jauntier than me, a real force of nature, but I was doing my best.

Bastion joined us the second we stepped outside. When we slid into the car and shut the doors, I let out a sharp breath of relief. I am *not* made to be a cat burglar. Now to discover the contents of that brown envelope…

Chapter 30

My hands were still useless. I'd never had them shake before, thank goodness; a witch whose hands trembled under pressure would make a lousy runemaster. Still, breaking and entering wasn't usually on my roster so I tried to forgive myself.

I was just about to tear open the brown envelope when my phone rang: Benji. I swiped to answer and noted with satisfaction that the trembling had already stopped. 'Benji, are you okay?'

'I'm fine Am Bam,' he said cheerfully. 'I've located Tarone. I have eyes on him right now. What do you want me to do?'

'Keep following him. I'm on my way, but it'll take three or four hours to drive to you. Don't lose him.'

'No, ma'am.' He hung up without any more pleasantries. That is one of the reasons I love him: he is efficient.

'The illusion is gone,' Bastion said with an odd note of relief in his voice. 'You're back to you.'

'Goddess, that was close.'

'Too close,' Oscar agreed.

I cleared my throat. 'We've got a lead on Tarone. Benji's found him.'

'You could fly, either on me or in a helicopter,' Bastion suggested. 'It would be quicker.'

I pointed to Oscar. 'We can't both fly on you, not comfortably.'

A smile tugged at Bastion's lips and he slid next to me in the car. 'I'm just letting you know that you're more than welcome to get your leg over me any time.'

In the front of the car, Oscar snorted quietly. My cheeks flushed. I met Bastion's eyes as bravely as I could and smiled a little, just to acknowledge his flirtation and to let him know that it was welcome even if I didn't have the first clue how to reciprocate. Anyway, acknowledging was probably fine – we didn't have to *act* on it. Baby steps.

Bastion's eyes heated and he gave the tiniest nod. His lips turned up a fraction, his equivalent of a wide, beaming grin.

I opened the brown envelope. As excellent as my self-control is, I had to know about the contents. It held a CD. 'Damn,' I huffed. 'Who puts information on a CD these days?'

'It was all the rage for a while,' Bastion noted.

'Yeah,' I muttered. 'Just after floppy discs were a thing.' I rubbed a hand over my face. 'My laptop doesn't even have a CD drive.'

Bastion slipped his phone out. 'I'll arrange for one to be delivered to our hotel.'

'Where are we staying? The Sheraton again?'

He shook his head. 'No, that was compromised.' He hesitated. 'There was some evidence our room was searched.'

'What? When?'

'When we were at the pyre.'

'Why didn't you say anything?'

'There was no need to worry you. I had the hotel change the keycard again and arranged for some extra security, but I decided that we may as well up the ante. As such, I've secured us rooms at The Witchery.'

My mouth dropped open. 'Isn't that even more compromised? Like putting our heads inside a crocodile's mouth?'

'It's time to increase the pressure,' Bastion said grimly. 'I don't like this cat-and-mouse bullshit. Benji has installed some cameras in the upstairs section of The Witchery so we have extra eyes. Shirdal is joining us up there, and Haiku is taking over guarding your mum with Charlize.'

'Haiku?'

'He's a good soldier and he and Charlize work well together,' he reassured me. 'Your mum will be safe. And,' he added pointedly, 'so will you.'

It was a nice promise, but I'd long been used to people letting me down. My dad's exodus had taught me to be self-sufficient. It is one of the reasons I am a pretty bad team player; I can't be let down by a teammate if there is only me on the team.

I'd been trying to ease up recently – letting Ethan and Jeb run things in my absence was a huge step for me. Normally I'd be logging in remotely and working every hour to make sure that everything was still going smoothly. There'd definitely been some personal growth.

'Okay,' I said. 'Let's do it. How do we bait the trap?'

'We let the killer think we've found something incriminating in Abigay's room, then wait to see who comes sniffing.'

'That presupposes we know who the killer is,' I pointed out drily.

'You have some idea who it might be. You're just not sharing.'

My list of suspects was woefully short, but he was right: I had one suspect. I've always held my cards close to my chest, and it was too much now to expect me to lay them on the table. But yes, I was almost certain who the killer was. I wanted to be wrong, though, because thinking I was right sent me into such a towering rage that all reason fled. I couldn't afford that now.

So instead I focused on what we were driving towards. It was time to meet Benji and speak to the evasive Tarone.

Chapter 31

We met Benji at the top of Frederick Street. Oscar stayed in the car, ready to make a quick getaway if we needed to.

Benji looked up as we approached then covered the distance between us. He drew me into a huge hug. 'Am Bam!' he greeted me happily. 'I've missed you.'

'And I you,' I admitted as I stood on tiptoe and kissed his cold, smooth cheek.

He drew back, beaming. I watched in surprise as he then barrelled into Bastion and gave *him* an enormous hug. Bastion looked a little nonplussed.

Benji drew back suddenly and his smile dropped as Bastion failed to respond. 'Is that not okay?' he asked. 'I've heard that a friend of a friend is a friend. And Amber is my friend and you are Amber's friend, so that must mean that we are friends. Is that not right?' His eyebrow ridges drew together.

I waited with bated breath for Bastion's response. If he crushed Benji, I would kill him no matter his strength.

Bastion stared at the golem. 'I don't have any friends besides Amber.'

Benji started to withdraw but Bastion's hand shot out and clamped around his wrist. 'But I would like to change that.'

Benji's smile was like the sun rising as Bastion drew him into a firm hug. My eyes stung – it must have been the dust in the air. When the men had stopped having their moment, I cleared my throat. 'So? Tarone?'

'He's in here!' Benji pointed to a little café a few yards away.

Greenwoods is a lovely café not far from the centre of Edinburgh. It has a red storefront and inside it has a sparkly tiled floor and a clean modern interior. Tarone was sitting just inside the door. It was mid-afternoon and the café was having a lull before closing. The staff were sweeping and tidying and cleaning, preparing to shut for the day.

'I'm sorry, food service has ended,' one of the waitresses told me, doing a good job of looking regretful rather than impatient.

'That's okay. We won't be long. Can I grab a cappuccino?'

'Of course. And for you?' She looked at the men.

'Orange juice,' Benji ordered happily.

'Nothing for me, thank you,' Bastion murmured.

Tarone looked up and froze like a rabbit in headlights. A golem and a griffin were an intimidating sight so I didn't blame him.

Before he could do something stupid like try to flee, I sat opposite him and the two men sat on the other free sides of the table. 'Hello, Tarone,' I said calmly. 'I've been phoning you but you haven't returned my calls.'

He folded his arms. 'That's not a crime, DeLea.'

'Nobody said it was – but it's interesting that your brain goes straight to criminality.'

He glared. 'My sister is dead. Have some respect.'

'I have plenty. I have nothing but respect for your sister and everything she accomplished with her life.'

'She would still be alive if she hadn't left Jamaica,' he said thickly, suddenly looking like a brother who was truly grieving.

'We can't know that.' I softened my tone. 'She made her choices and she loved her life.'

'But not her family,' he huffed.

'That's not true and you know it,' I said vehement-ly. 'She sent gifts to the family every birthday and every Christmas. She did video calls with your children and their children, too.'

'But she didn't visit,' he grumped.

'Because she feared you wouldn't let her return to Eng-land.' I wasn't going to pussyfoot around; he had made Abigay feel like that. If she hadn't returned to Jamaica, it was only him that was to blame.

His shoulders slumped and he stirred his tea dejectedly. 'I know,' he murmured.

'Did you see her before she died?' I asked. I knew that he had but if he lied about it...

He nodded. 'Yes, I went to her home. We had tea and scones and cakes together. She loves ... *loved* afternoon tea. She always had a sweet tooth.' His eyes grew misty as he reminisced.

'What did you talk about?'

He sighed. 'I've aged. My daughter Donya tells me that I've been living in the past, that my fears have been pushing Abigay away. That it is *my* attitude that is the problem, not hers.'

He lifted his eyes to mine. 'My daughter informs me that she is a lesbian. She has known for fifteen years. *Fifteen years.* It took her this long to tell me. Donya's "best friend" Delyse "Bunnyhop" Johnson has been with her for five years. They live together – I always thought it was to save money on rent. Bunnyhop has come to dinner on many occasions.'

He closed his eyes. 'And I've been talking to my wife about when Donya would finally find a husband.' He groaned aloud in mortification.

'Donya told Abigay she was gay, and Abigay was never less than supportive. I thanked her for that. It was an emotional talk,' he admitted. 'I said I felt like I was failing as a father because Donya hadn't been able to speak to me or my wife. Abigay said it is only a failure when you give up.'

Tarone looked up. 'I'm going to do better. It's not too late to change. Donya only told me because she and Bunnyhop are going to have a baby together – they've done IVF. I have a grandbaby on the way.'

'Congratulations,' I said honestly.

He gave me a shaky smile. 'Abigay promised to come home at Christmas and meet the new baby. And now she never will.' Tears filled his eyes. He looked away and inhaled sharply through his nose, trying to keep them from falling. 'Donya has already said that if the baby is a girl, she'll be named Abigay after her aunt.'

I swallowed past the rock in my throat. 'That's lovely.'

He nodded jerkily. 'I let Abigay down, and now I don't have the chance to right those wrongs.'

'Right them with Donya and her child. Abigay wasn't one to hold a grudge.'

'No, but I am.' He gave a wry smile. 'It's another of my faults. I'm trying to change that, but there's one thing I want to be clear on – I'll never forgive her killer. You'll find them, won't you?'

'I will,' I promised, and I meant it with all my heart. Failure wasn't an option, nor was it a word in my lexicon.

I *would* find her killer. Nothing would stop me.

222

Chapter 32

We left the cosy café and walked together to the car.

'Bunnyhop is an unusual name,' Benji remarked.

'It's a nickname,' I explained. 'In Jamaica they call them "yard names". Abigay's yard name was "Salad" because whenever she went to a cookout, she always went straight for the salad.'

'You knew her well,' he noted.

'She half-raised me, especially when I got older. Mum was working hard to make ends meet and raise funds to send me to Edinburgh for my mastery, but she didn't want my rune work to slacken in the meantime so she got Abigay to tutor me.'

Benji wrapped an arm around me. 'You must be sad. Friends comfort friends when they are sad.'

I leaned into him. 'They do. I *am* sad, but mostly I'm mad. When the mad goes, the sadness will stay.'

'Abigay was very old, so that makes it better, doesn't it?' he asked hopefully. 'I have heard people say things like "it was her time" and "she lived a good life".'

'Whilst that is true, it doesn't make her loss any easier to bear. We humans have a lot of loss in our lives, and we have to do something to make it easier to cope with, so we utter these empty platitudes to each other. But they don't make the loss better. Nothing does, but no one likes feeling helpless.' I cleared my throat. 'And you only think she's old because you're what? Twenty, now?'

He held up two beefy fingers. 'Twenty-two.'

'Where has the time gone?' I gave him one last squeeze and stepped away. 'Shall we head back to The Witchery?'

My phone beeped with a text from Peter, my dragon-shifter potion ingredient grower: *Sorry that it has taken so long to compile this. Here is a list of witches that have recently and regularly purchased felfa leaves. I compiled it with the help of other felfa growers I am friendly with. There are more growers with whom I am not friendly so the list is not exhaustive.*

Exhaustive or not, it was depressingly long. I scrolled through it and noted a number of my suspects including Eleanora, Hilary and Beatrice. Certainty settled into my gut but I needed evidence; at the moment I had nothing but my suspicions. Bastion was right: I had to set a trap.

'Anything you wish to share with class?' Bastion asked, making me smile a little. I passed him my phone so he could read the screen.

'Felfa?' he asked, quirking an eyebrow.

'It's used to make various healing potions, but it's also one of the rarest ingredients in black mordis.'

'But everyone on this list could be completely innocent?'

'Absolutely.' I grimaced. 'It's not the smoking gun we need.' I'd hoped for a shorter list.

Bastion studied me. 'You look like you've made a decision. Your main suspect is on this list?'

I nodded.

Benji didn't ask to see the list and I didn't share it with him because his oath-enforced allegiance to the Council would be problematic. Even so, I didn't want to cut him out of the investigation and send him back to the dank underground if I didn't have to.

I slid my eyes to him and Bastion followed my gaze. He gave a slight nod then changed the subject. 'Tarone could use a crying jag.'

'Shall we send him a copy of *The Notebook*?' I asked drily. 'That sure worked for me.'

'Maybe *My Sister's Keeper* would work better for him just now.'

I'd watched that movie once before but I'd started crying before the opening credits even started. 'That's just cruel!' I joked.

We reached the car and slid into it. 'To The Witchery,' Bastion instructed Oscar.

The short drive didn't take long. I used the time to text a few of the witches on my suspect list, including my main one. I confirmed that we'd found some evidence of black magic in Abigay's room and that Bastion would secure the room until such time as the Council could remove the dark artefacts. I postulated that Abigay had found the trinkets on her tour of the covens and she'd removed them for safekeeping. The trap was set and baited.

Oscar parked up in the witches' car park and we walked the rest of the way on foot. As always, Rosemary was on duty front of house. She gaped as I went in. 'Amber! Where have you been? You were summoned by the Council this morning!'

I could hardly explain that I'd been doing some breaking and entering in Liverpool. My eyes narrowed. 'I haven't received a summons.'

'You must have!' Her eyes were wide with distress. 'They sent out alerts to all potential candidates.'

I checked my phone again: nothing from the Council. 'Potential candidates for what?'

'For testing! For the Symposium member position.' She bit her lip. 'You'd better run. If they start the tests without you, you'll be ineligible.'

Shit!

I grabbed Bastion's arm and pulled him away from Rosemary's listening ears. 'I baited the trap,' I explained hurriedly. 'Terrible timing. You'll have to stay here to see who comes.'

'I'm not leaving you,' he refused flatly, crossing his arms.

I glared at him. 'You have to. I'm not letting this opportunity pass us by.'

'We have cameras. They'll have to be enough.'

'Well, they're not,' I snapped. 'We need to catch them in the act, not loitering in the hallway. We don't have cameras in Abigay's room, do we?' He shook his head. 'So one of us has to be here to ambush the black witch, and it needs to be you. You can take them out.'

'I am here to protect you,' Bastion said stubbornly. 'That is my sole duty. I am not leaving you.'

'Leaving me is protecting me! This is our opportunity to catch the black witch who's targeting me.'

'You know as well as I do that there's a whole coven of them. Capturing one of them won't make you any safer.'

'I'll stay here,' Oscar said firmly, interrupting our bickering. 'And I'll summon all of you if someone starts poking around. Amber, you have to go! If you miss this chance it may never come again.'

He wasn't wrong but I felt conflicted leaving him to face a black witch alone. 'You won't confront her, right? Just get evidence she was there?'

'Right. Now GO!'

I went. I prayed I wouldn't regret my decision.

Chapter 33

We were running through the underground city. 'Too slow!' Benji grunted. 'Do you trust me, Am?'

'Of course I trust you!'

'Good.' He looked at Bastion. 'Meet us at the examination room. I will guard her until then. You have my word and oath.' Then he swept me into his arms and walked us into the walls. I started to scream but shut my mouth abruptly as the walls met my face.

To say the experience of travelling through the walls was terrifying is an understatement. Somehow I could feel every grain of mud and sand passing through my being as Benji propelled us forward. We were moving faster than a rollercoaster, and if I'd had any air in my lungs I'd have been screaming. It felt like a second and a lifetime. When he finally burst us out of the walls, I bent double and sucked in a couple of desperate breaths.

'Hurry!' Benji urged. 'They're starting!' He gave me no time to recover, just opened the huge wooden doors in front of me and shoved me in. 'Amber DeLea presents herself!' he called into the cavernous room.

This wasn't the coven Council's chambers but the witches' hall. The full Council was sitting and before them were a number of witches: Kassandra Scholes, Eleanora Moonspell, Beatrice Wraithborne, Jason Bivane and Harold Tipither.

Jason and Harold weren't real contenders, even if they didn't know it. Harold had a rich dad but the magical ability and concentration span of a possessed mouse. He hadn't mastered any of the witches' core subjects. Jason had plenty of knowledge and ambition, but he was far too young. He'd only passed his runes' mastery two years earlier and had yet to be tried and tested. Kass had her potions' mastery, as did Eleanora, and both of them were strong contenders – but I was the only one who had mastered potions *and* runes.

Beatrice was a surprise. I'd thought she was gunning for the Crone role but perhaps this was her backup option.

'I apologise,' I said demurely to the room at large, like I wasn't hopping mad at the omission. 'I didn't receive a notification of the testing.'

There were murmurs between the councillors. They all had their faces hidden by shadows and that suddenly gave me the chills. What if the shadows hid more than their face? How could we know that the Council members were who they claimed to be? The last few times they'd met, they'd had their cowls up. Abigay had said that wasn't usual, yet the cowls were all I'd seen. What if an imposter was lurking amongst them?

The thought was like ice in my veins but there was nothing I could do about it right at that minute. Throwing accusations about would torpedo my chances of the membership seat faster than you could say 'sunken ship'.

I sat at one of the examination tables and did my best to focus on the paper in front of me.

'Pssst,' Eleanora hissed at me.

I looked at her. 'What?'

'Why did you text me about dark artefacts?' A frown passed over her worn face.

'I might need some help nullifying them,' I lied.

Her expression cleared. 'Oh well, I can help with that. You need plenty of avronda root. I know a guy.'

So did I. I nodded and studied her eyes but there was nothing in them but simple curiosity: no zeal, no covetous light. She wasn't interested in the artefacts for herself.

Eleanora had always been at the bottom of my suspect list and now I scratched her off.

I looked at the cloaked and hooded figures around me. Amongst them were Hilary and Willow. Hilary had been one of Abigay's best friends; she was also my chief suspect.

With all of the Council members here, I didn't have to worry about Oscar back at The Witchery. If Hilary was here, she wouldn't be attacking Oscar for the black artefacts. He was safe. Something in me eased and I focused on the test in front of me.

I turned over the top paper and smiled a little as I saw runes. If this whole test was rune based, I was a shoo-in.

Unfortunately, the rune paper was followed by a mystic paper with crystal-ball uses. That isn't my speciality; I prefer to leave that sort of thing to the seers. I know the basics because I have to teach them to the acolytes, but it isn't my passion. Divining the future is always a tricky business and it has the potential to ruin lives. I'd seen too many self-fulfilling prophecies to dabble lightly.

After that there was a potion theory paper, which I no doubt excelled at, and then a potion practical. When I finally looked up to take a breath, our coven Council audience had dwindled to just three. With their hoods up, I didn't know which three were left – and I had no way of knowing if Hilary was amongst them. My stomach lurched in panic. Oscar!

I looked towards Bastion. He was on his phone, looking at me. He shook his head and hung up. His face was carefully blank, but Benji looked worried. I chewed my bottom lip. Something was happening and I'd bet my bottom dollar it was happening at The Witchery.

What mattered more to me: Oscar's safety or my lifelong dream of becoming a member of the Symposium?

In the end, it was a no-brainer.

Chapter 34

'What are you doing?' one of the hooded Council members said as I stood up from my desk and walked away from the potion ingredients.

'I have somewhere I need to be,' I said flatly.

'Amber, if you walk away without completing the last test, we can't make you the Symposium member.' I recognised Willow's American twang.

'I know, Willow. It's okay. Thank you for all your help in getting me this far.'

'You didn't need my help, Amber. You deserve to be here.'

I smiled. 'Thank you for that. I appreciate it.'

Kass was watching me with wide eyes. She pointed urgently back to my place, her meaning clear. I smiled ruefully and shook my head. 'Good luck,' I mouthed.

With worry for Oscar churning my gut, I ran to Benji and Bastion. 'Let's go.' Neither of them argued with me as we started running through the underground city.

'Here,' Benji rumbled. 'You can break through here. I'll mend the damage afterwards so no one will know. I'll travel through the walls and meet you in Abigay's room.'

The ceiling above us looked solid and we eyed him dubiously. Benji punched it hard; his fist didn't go through it but *into* it. Then he yanked hard and the whole thing came raining down on us. Bastion shifted into griffin form and threw open his wings to protect us from the falling debris.

Benji looked at us sheepishly. 'I used a little too much power there.'

'No? Really?' Bastion snarked.

I elbowed him. 'It's fine.' I smiled at Benji. 'Thank you for making the opening. Are you sure you can close it?'

'Easily,' Benji assured me. 'Go. I'll meet you there.'

Since Bastion was in his griffin form, we might as well use it. I climbed onto his back. 'Get us to The Witchery,' I ordered.

'Hold on,' he grunted back.

I grabbed a tuft of fur at the apex of his back and clung on for dear life. His huge wings beat around us and drew us upwards. In moments we were airborne.

Benji knew what he was doing: he'd hustled us through the underground city so that we weren't far from The Witchery. Bastion's wings beat up and away and in less than a minute we were landing on the roof. He shimmered back into human form as I slid from his back, then took point as we ran down to the floor below.

Oscar was in the corridor outside Abigay's room. He looked up as we approached and relief washed over his features. 'It's Hilary,' he whispered, disbelievingly. 'It's Hilary in there. I don't understand. She *loved* Abigay.'

I grimaced. 'We'll have plenty of time to ask her about it. Oscar, put your mobile in your breast pocket with the camera facing outwards – we'll need evidence to take to the Council. Let's go talk to this witch with a b.'

Bastion's lips twitched. 'It would be far more effective if you just said bitch.'

'Swearing is the sign of a small mind,' I said primly.

'Not swearing is the sign of a prude,' he countered.

'I'm not a prude!'

'Children,' Oscar interjected, his phone in place. 'Now isn't the time to bicker.'

'I'm no child,' Bastion glared at Oscar.

'And yet you're acting like one. Shall we?' He gestured to the door. 'Potential black witch inside, remember?'

I remembered. I'd been putting off this moment since it had first occurred to me how Abigay had really died. The nail in the coffin had been the text from Peter. Now it was time to give Hilary enough rope so she could hang herself.

We were about to open the door when Benji slid out of the walls. I suppressed a scream of shock. 'We need to give you bells around your neck or something,' I muttered.

'They wouldn't help,' Benji pointed out. 'They wouldn't ring in the walls.'

'I don't suppose they would,' I agreed. 'Right, now we have a full team, is everyone ready?'

They nodded. 'Let's go in all smiles and take it from there.'

We opened the door. The room looked like a bomb had gone off: the bed had literally been torn apart and the mattress had a great rip down it as if Hilary had been searching for something inside it. She was near the wall where she'd just finished painting a rune, *ezro*. She'd cancelled something too, but it had already dissipated so I didn't know what. I'd have to touch the wall and examine the runes to find out exactly what she'd cancelled but time was against me, so instead I turned to her.

'Hello, Hilary,' I said, keeping my voice light and welcoming. 'What are you doing here?' Like the bed being torn apart wasn't a huge giveaway that something nefarious was at play.

She looked up and took us all in, and I saw the moment she decided to try and talk her way out of this one. It was going to be difficult with the torn-up mattress, but I welcomed her effort to try.

She went on the offensive. 'What are you doing here, child?' she asked, hands on hips. 'You can't have completed the examination already!'

'No, I left early. It turns out that other things are more important than tests.'

'It's not the tests that are important but the position. Think of all the good you could do as the member of the Symposium!' Her eyes were wide with entreaty; good effort, Hilary, but I didn't buy it.

'If it's so good, why didn't you apply?' I asked coolly. 'Beatrice was sitting in the examination hall with me.'

Hilary waved that away. 'Oh, I'm not one for tests. I've no need to prove myself to anyone.'

'And besides,' I said pointedly, 'it's the Crone position that you covet, isn't it?'

Her narrowed. 'I don't like your tone. What are you implying, Amber?'

'I'm not implying anything. I'm saying that you want to be the next Crone, don't you?'

She pressed her lips into a thin line. 'I am keen to progress Abigay's excellent work.'

'No doubt.' Impatience raced through me; I've never been one to pussyfoot around so I said bluntly, 'It would be a lot easier for the black coven if they had a black witch responsible for hunting them down.'

The effect of my words was instantaneous: a potion bomb and an athame were in her hands.

Maybe I should have been more subtle after all.

Chapter 35

'What gave me away?' Hilary asked calmly as her eyes leached to black. Oh heck. She was using necromancy – runeless so the connection would be weak – but even so.

'Your first mistake was the diary,' I explained. 'It gnawed at me because Abigay didn't keep diaries; she kept everything in her head. So why would you suggest she had one unless it was a red herring to send us haring off on a quest to find non-existent books?'

'Which you did not fall for,' she groused.

'No,' I agreed. 'I knew Abigay so I never wasted time on the fake books, but that was the moment I started looking at you. Your next mistake? The wards weren't compromised. The more I thought about it, the less sense it made that they'd been broken in some way that I didn't recognise. I'm a rune *master*. Abigay's wards were perfect and they hadn't been breached because nobody had attacked her in her sleep, as you'd suggested.

'Moonspell confirmed that you didn't go to the ceilidh as you'd told Abigay. You went home, where I suspect you brewed some fresh black mordis. You came to Abigay's house that morning, not with a healing potion but with your freshly brewed poison. You painted it on her, all the while acting like you were trying to paint *ezro* to cancel a rune you hadn't even painted on her yet. She was thanking you when you were painting *angrepet* on her.'

I broke off as fury washed over me with such strength that tears sprang to my eyes. But angry crying was useless and I dashed away the tears.

'I noted the similarities in the rune style at the time, but I dismissed it as coincidence. You loved Abigay so it couldn't be you. But the more I thought about it, the more sense it made. That's why it took her "so long" to die from black mordis; one of the fastest acting poisons known. She didn't survive all night and morning, as you suggested. It didn't take her long to succumb to the poison because you'd painted the rune *that* morning, then you deceived her into believing someone had broken in and painted *angrepet* while she was asleep.' Fury washed over me again. 'She was your *friend!* How could you?'

Hilary sighed and for a moment she looking tired and worn. 'You don't get a whole lot of autonomy in the black coven, Amber. I protected Abigay for years as best I could. She always told me which coven she was visiting so I could give a heads up to our operatives. I worked hard to stop her finding evidence of black magic in this coven or that, or I buried her reports so that no one would see them. But she started to wonder why her findings weren't being investigated. She was asking too many questions. The orders came from on high that she had to be removed.' She grimaced. 'It made sense,' she said reluctantly.

'Killing your friend never makes sense.'

'And how would you know?' she spat back. 'You don't have friends. Your little father figure is the sole friend in your life, and that's it. He pities you.' She gestured to Oscar.

Oscar shook his head once, but his focus was internal, on his magic. His lighter was in his hands, ready to be flicked on. He was waiting to hear Hilary out – but he was ready to set her on fire if she attempted to hurt me with that wicked-looking athame.

Benji spoke up. 'She has friends. She has me.'

'Lucky her.' Hilary smirked unkindly. 'A hunk of clay she made into a boy likes her.'

'Don't you dare talk about Benji like that!' I snarled. 'He is worth his weight in gold.'

'Oh, he is,' she agreed. 'To the right person. Luckily, that person is me. His obedience to the Council is absolute.' She fixed her eyes on him triumphantly. 'Benji, kill Bastion.'

Benji visibly fought the order but his eyes glowed white as it seized him and his hands shifted into sharp spikes. 'Run, Bastion!' he cried to his new friend as he advanced unwillingly on him.

'Don't you dare hurt him!' I shouted to Bastion. 'Don't you hurt him!' Bastion's jaw clenched but he nodded.

'I can't help it,' Benji whimpered, thinking I was talking to him. Then he charged forward towards Bastion.

And that's when the vampyrs phased in.

Chapter 36

There were three of them, their eyes were black, and Hilary had them under her complete control. Now I knew which rune she'd been cancelling: the anti-vampyr one.

One flew at Oscar, who used his fire straight away. Even as his skin burned, the vampyr continued his assault but I had to turn my attention away because I had my own attacker to contend with. I tried to grab the athame from my ankle holster but the vampyr moved too fast. In a blink he was on me, teeth bared and ready to bite.

He threw himself towards my exposed neck – but just as suddenly he was thrown back. My protective runes had kicked in.

I used the momentary breathing room to grab my athame. I was fumbling it to chest height when I caught my finger on the blade and it bit into my flesh. The scent of blood wafted in the air. The vampyr that was attacking me was clearly struggling against his necromantic bonds – desperation was painted across his face – and the scent of blood was the edge that he needed to push a little more. For a second his eyes flashed blue and in that moment, I saw him decide. He shoved himself forward onto my athame, piercing his heart with my blade before his eyes leached to black again.

My mouth dropped in horror as he slid off the athame. A moment later he disintegrated into ashes, truly dead. Vampyrs are notoriously difficult to kill, but it looked like my family heirloom packed a punch.

My hand trembled but I had no time to think about what had just happened. Oscar's vampyr was still fighting with him, but it would only be a matter of moments before he succumbed to the flames. Bastion's vampyr had already been beheaded and his head had landed a few feet away. How Bastion had managed that feat while dancing around to avoiding Benji's unwilling attacks was a mystery to me. As I watched, the vampyr's body and head turned to dust.

Benji was in front of me, his glowing white eyes fixed on Bastion. He stormed forward, slashing his powerful forearms. Bastion ducked and dived, rolling over the broken bed in a bid to get away from the golem, but he was hamstrung. He wasn't doing anything to hurt Benji, just trying to keep his distance as Benji came at him like Edward Scissorhands in a rage.

Rune ruin! Benji wouldn't stop until Bastion was dead unless another Council member ordered him to. I needed time, time to fetch a Council member that I trusted. As the number of obstacles in the room were destroyed, there was an increased risk that Benji and Bastion would do serious harm to each other. With Bastion trying so hard not to hurt Benji, I feared it would be the griffin's blood sprayed on the walls. How had I ever once wished for that to happen?

I had to power down Benji. My heart ached and tears filled my eyes. There was a chance that doing that would wipe his personality from him. I prayed with all my heart that he would stay with us, but if I delayed one of the men would die. At least this way there was a chance that both of them would live.

'I'm sorry, Benji,' I cried as I stepped forward and painted *ezro* on the back of his head using the blood from my finger.

Benji held himself as still as he could, fighting the compulsion to attack Bastion to give me the ten seconds I needed to paint the rune. He understood what I was doing and his blessing was implicit. My heart broke that he was helping me to save Bastion at the risk of his own life.

'I'm sorry!' I cried again as I pulsed my magic through the inelegant rune. As it activated, Benji slumped over and his head dropped to his chest. His huge form started to topple forward but Bastion hastily leapt over the bed to catch him whilst still avoiding his sharp blades. If Benji fell on the floor, there was a chance he would shatter.

Behind me, Hilary sighed. 'I have to do everything myself,' she bitched as she stepped forward. She drew back her athame and I saw her intention a split second before it happened. 'Bastion!' I screamed in warning.

Bastion was trapped under the weight of Benji and he moved too slowly.

Hilary's blade cut into his gut, then she pulled back the blade and stabbed him again. I was moving before I even thought about it. A potion bomb in the confines of this room would kill us all, so I swung my athame wildly at her. I meant to scare or injure her; perhaps to give her a wound like she had given to Bastion, and I expected her to fight me off. But her blade was buried in Bastion so she offered no defence as my athame swung towards her. I watched in horror as my sharp blade sliced through the soft skin of her throat.

'Oh fuck,' I swore, eyes wide as her blood bubbled up and sprayed me.

Her hands reached up to her broken skin and she looked at me in disbelief. She tried to talk but her vocal chords had been sliced; her lips moved but no words came out. Then she held my gaze as she slowly slumped to the floor, eyes glassy and wide.

She was dead, at my hands. I had a moment to stare at the blood on my fingers before my brain switched on and started working; this was no time for self-pity.

'Bastion!' I dropped my athame from numb fingers and hurried to where he was still pinned under Benji.

A window shattered behind me; if it was more vampyrs then I was a goner. I whirled around, fingering the potion bomb. If they were close enough to the window, maybe I could throw it at them without killing us all.

Luckily, it was Shirdal. 'Here I come to save the day,' the head of the griffins declared as he looked around the room. 'Oh,' he said, disappointed. 'The day already seems to have been saved. That's a shame. I was looking forward to some good old-fashioned murder and mayhem.' He sighed.

'Help me!' I begged him. 'Get Benji off Bastion!'

'Benji?'

'The golem!'

There was a shriek and in flew Fehu. He screamed as he frantically flew around the ceiling, kraaing in distress. Then he shot down, landed on my shoulder and nipped at my ear. Ouch! The little bastard had drawn blood in his urgency.

'I know! I know!' I shouted. 'I'm helping him! One moment, Fehu!'

Shirdal and I strained beneath Benji's weight as we slowly drew him to his feet.

'He's going to fall over again,' Shirdal grunted. Because Benji had been mid-step when he'd powered down, we couldn't stand him upright, so we leaned him back instead and propped him carefully against the wall.

I turned back to Bastion. 'Shift!' I ordered. His shift could heal virtually all cuts. It was why the bastards made such good assassins: they were virtually indestructible as long as they didn't get hit with a death blow.

Bastion didn't reply. He was unconscious, incapable of anything – including shifting. Fuck. 'Get my bag!' I screamed at Oscar. 'Hurry!'

Bastion's lifeblood was pouring onto the hard wooden floor.

Chapter 37

I ripped my skirt into pieces, using it to try and staunch the gaping wounds, but in seconds the material was sodden. There was too much blood, far too much. Bastion's tanned skin was pale, and I had never once told him how I felt. That I liked him. *Liked him* liked him. And now I would never get the chance. 'Bastion, don't you dare die on me. We have unfinished business, you hear me?' I begged.

Oscar came in, panting, and threw my tote bag towards me. I caught it and ripped it open then hesitated for a second: a healing potion or a transformative one? In the end I went for the latter because the shift would heal Bastion's body. I painted on the runes and let my magic pour through them. I wasn't trying to be subtle.

Nothing happened. 'Why isn't it working?' I cried.

Oscar picked up Hilary's athame, examined the hilt and smelled the blade. 'Poisoned and cursed,' he pronounced.

Fuck, fuck, fuckity-fuck.

There was only one potion that would save him now and it wasn't one that was in my tote bag. I rooted through Bastion's pockets, desperately searching for the small black bottle that carried his final defence potion. Each griffin had one vial so he *had* to have one – but his pockets were empty. Where the hell was it?

'Where is your final defence?' I shouted at my unconscious bodyguard.

'He gave it to Jessica Sharpe,' Shirdal murmured.

'What?' My brain kicked in. 'Then give him yours!'

Shirdal hesitated, just for a beat. 'Please!' I begged. 'I'll make a whole new batch. I'll give you another vial within a matter of days. Please, Shirdal!'

He grimaced but reached into his pocket and pulled out a small round vial no bigger than my thumb. I unstoppered it, pried open Bastion's mouth and poured it in, then shut his mouth and held my hand over it so he couldn't spit it out. I stroked his throat to make him swallow reflexively and I nearly sobbed when he did.

I watched his wounds; when they started to close I let the tears fall. Thank the Goddess. I dashed away the tears and fought to pull myself together. His wounds were all but gone, and in another moment not even a mark would remain. Virtually nothing could stand against a final defence potion – it was a shame that there was no human equivalent because the potion for the griffins was a wonder to behold. And when I got home I was going to brew the biggest vat of it so I could load Bastion's pockets full of the precious vials.

Bastion didn't stir awake like a normal person; one moment he was unconscious and the next his eyes snapped open. 'All clear,' Shirdal said straight away and Bastion's tense body relaxed.

He looked around, assessing the scene. 'Hilary?' he asked. He couldn't see her body from where he was lying.

'Ding-dong, the witch is dead,' Shirdal quipped.

'Benji?'

'He's powered down,' I confessed. 'We'll need to do a ritual to awaken him.' I pressed my lips together. 'There's a chance he won't wake properly, not as the Benji we know. I had to shut him down too fast.'

Bastion sat up. 'He'll be fine,' he reassured me. 'He's a fighter. He beheaded the vampyr that was attacking me. Even while Benji was advancing on me, he was still trying to help me, to fight the order to kill me.'

'He's a good friend,' I sniffed, my eyes blurring again. I didn't have so many friends that I could afford to lose one, and the thought of Benji never waking again filled me with a cold horror that I would never be able to shake. If I had done this to him and he didn't wake, I'd never forgive myself.

'Hey,' Bastion tipped my chin up so I met his brown eyes. 'He's going to be okay. Just you wait and see.'

I nodded but I didn't really believe it.

Bastion moved his hands apart; just the tiniest of motions, but it was enough of an invitation for a hug for me to barrel into him. He wrapped his arms around me and I breathed in the scent of him.

'Well now,' Shirdal murmured smugly. 'It seems like things have changed between you two. About time, Bastion.'

I ignored his snarky comment. Bastion was alive. If Shirdal hadn't been there... I shuddered to think of the hole in my life that Bastion would have left if he'd died. In only a matter of a few weeks, he'd forced me to re-examine my preconceived notions about him. He had saved me from kelpies and bombs and rogue fire elementals and more, throwing himself in harm's way again and again. He had slept under my bed when I was scared, he had brought me romance books, smiled at my stupid mugs, made me pancakes as he danced in my kitchen, and he had cried with me while we watched *The Notebook* together. He was more to me than I'd ever thought possible and I'd nearly lost him. Lost him before I'd even had a chance to *have* him.

Luckily, I'm a witch that always learns from her mistakes.

Chapter 38

I looked at the total mess of Abigay's room and felt a twinge of guilt for turning her haven into a battleground. There were three large piles of vampyrs' remains with a fourth smaller one a little way off – the vampyr's head.

Hilary lay where she'd fallen and I wasn't inclined to move her. Shirdal briskly searched her and turned up another cursed athame and a few black potions that I confiscated into my tote. I wrapped the pair of daggers in the strips of my skirt that I hadn't used on Bastion and tucked them into my bag, too. Luckily, I was wearing my ever-present leggings under the remains of my skirt, though I felt oddly naked without the swish around my ankles.

'Nice look,' Shirdal commented.

I glared at him and tore off the rest of my skirt. 'Oscar, did you get the footage?' I asked urgently, sweeping my eyes over him for any sign of injury. I relaxed when there was none. Old or not, Oscar still had it.

He looked at his phone – he'd stopped recording when he'd returned with my tote bag – and grimaced as he flicked through the footage. 'We can hear Hilary confess but a lot of what followed was obscured by the flaming vampyr. He kept going a lot longer than I expected.'

'The confession is all we need to prove to the Council that it was a lawful kill. Email me a copy?'

He nodded and tapped at his phone.

'Okay.' I scrubbed at my face. 'We need to take Benji back down into the underground city and revive him, then tell the Council what happened. Can you two carry him?'

'Easy,' Shirdal said, though it definitely wouldn't be. I knew from my brief wrestle with Benji that he was no featherweight.

'What kept you?' Bastion asked Shirdal.

'I was half way to you when Charlize summoned me.' He turned to me. 'Your mum was attacked.'

My heart froze. 'What?!'

'She's fine,' he reassured me hastily. 'But we've relocated her.'

'To where?'

'A griffin safe house. Haiku and Charlize are with her.'

'What attacked her?'

'A wizard,' he said grimly. 'Wearing a Connection uniform.'

My blood ran cold. 'Why was he there?'

Shirdal grimaced. 'Charlize wasn't keen on a Q&A session. She killed him and secured your mum. Once I saw your mother ensconced in the safe house, I came back to join you.'

'She needs her medicines and her carers,' Oscar said in panic.

'Charlize took her medicines and the carers wrote her a list of instructions. She'll take good care of Luna,' Shirdal promised. 'She's got quite friendly with her, actually, and she took the attack quite personally.'

I blew out a breath and tried to calm myself. Mum was fine; she'd been attacked but she was *fine.* I reached out to Oscar and held his hand tightly for a moment, anchoring us both. 'Okay. She's okay.' I blew out a long breath.

'She is,' Shirdal promised. 'That's why I was late.'

'I'll forgive your tardiness,' Bastion growled playfully.

'You should,' I murmured absentmindedly. 'He gave you his final defence.'

Bastion froze, genuine shock written across his face. 'Shirdal?' he breathed. 'What did you do?'

Shirdal gave a nonchalant shrug. 'It's not a big deal, boy.'

'It is. You know it is. I don't have my final defence to give back to you.'

'I'll brew more,' I interrupted.

'The witches brew it every ten years and I'm sure it's only been eight or nine. Shirdal can't be one or two years without the final defence. He's our leader.'

Shirdal waved away Bastion's fears.

'I'll brew it,' I repeated. 'I got black kiteen from Peter. That's the rarest ingredient, everything else I can source. I might not be able to make a big batch with one leaf but I can make enough for a handful of vials, enough for you and Shirdal.'

Bastion's eyes were still wide as he reached out and lightly touched Shirdal on the arm. 'Thank you. *Sharmande kardin, Shirdal joon.*' I had no idea what language fell from his lips but I could tell that for Bastion, that was positively gushing.

Shirdal nodded once, clearly uncomfortable with the effusive gratitude. '*Khâhesh mikonam.*' He nodded at me. 'She was crying. You know how I hate to see a beautiful woman cry.' He tried to leer at me but his heart wasn't in it.

Bastion looked sharply at me. 'You were crying?' He sounded surprised.

I nodded shortly. 'We'll talk about it later. Now we need to sort out Benji.'

Both men nodded, business-like now. Bastion took Benji's shoulders and Shirdal took his feet. Getting him down the small winding staircase would be fun, but I trusted the griffins' spatial awareness. We could do it; we needed to.

I needed to bring Benji back to himself and every minute that passed made it less likely that would happen.

Chapter 39

I needed another witch, one that I could trust. At home I would have summoned Meredith, Jeb or Ethan, but here I had no one. Well, perhaps one.

I pulled out my phone and rang Kass. She answered almost immediately. 'Amber?' she sounded uncertain.

'I need your help. Can you come to the golem chambers? Third one off the right.' I looked around the creation chamber. Benji lay unmoving on the platform in the centre of the room and it looked wrong to see him so still. I had a flashback to Aunt Abigay lying in the same way and had to scrub my eyes to rid myself of the phantom vision. Benji was still, but he wasn't dead. Not yet.

'The creation chamber?' Kass sounded confused.

'Yes,' I confirmed urgently.

'Why are you—? Never mind.' She hesitated. 'Have you heard?'

'Heard what?'

She took a deep breath. 'I've been appoi
witch member of the Symposium.'

Crushing disappointment flooded through me. I
closed my eyes and willed myself not to cry, not when I
had witnesses. It was just a *job*, a job I'd wanted forever
but still just a job. Oscar was alive, and so were Bastion
and Benji – hopefully – and my mum. All of that was
far more important than a title.

'Congratulations,' I said. If my voice warbled a little,
I was sure she would forgive me.

'Thank you,' she whispered back. 'I'm sorry.'

I pushed aside my disappointment and refocused.
'Don't be. Can you still come and help me?'

'Of course I will! I'll excuse myself from the celebra-
tions and I'll come now.'

'Don't tell anyone where you're going,' I instructed.
'Hilary was a black witch.'

'What? Hilary Mitchell?' She gasped. A beat later she
asked, 'Was?'

'She's dead. She's the one who killed Abigay. She
confessed and I have it on camera.'

'By the Goddess,' Kass murmured. '*Hilary*? I can't believe it. I would have put money on her being the next Crone.'

'So would she,' I said grimly. 'She was counting on it, then she could use her position to hide the other black witches.'

'There are definitely more?' She sounded resigned.

'Yes.'

She swore at length. I interrupted her. 'Listen, I need your help. Now.'

'Sorry. It was a shock. I'm on my way.' Kass hung up.

I busied myself with the preparations. 'Remove his clothing,' I instructed Oscar and Bastion. I hoped Kass would run because I didn't want to delay any longer. Every second counted and I was desperate. I couldn't lose Benji, not on top of everything else I had to endure.

I carefully mixed the two volatile awakening potions and divided the mixture into two small cauldrons. I put one of them on what would be Kass's side of the table and the other on mine, then I dabbed my paintbrush with the mixture and waited impatiently. I was ready; I just needed a witch to mirror me.

Kass burst into the room. Her electric-blue backpack was slung over one shoulder and Jax over the other. 'Benjamin!' she cried when she spotted the prone golem.

'Hurry!' I barked. 'I've mixed the awakening potions. We mustn't delay.'

She dropped her bag, took her favourite brush out of it and dunked it in the cauldron of potion that was waiting for her.

'Ready? Three, two, one. Now,' I ordered.

We started to paint, matching rune for rune, her on one side of Benji's body and me on the other: *sowilo* for vitality; *uruz* for power; *ewhaz* for movement, and finally *gebo* for gift. We gifted our magic to Benji so he could wake up again.

It wasn't as complex as a full awakening because he was dormant rather than unmade. We painted rune after rune until every inch of the front of him was covered, even his feet. The griffins carefully turned him over and we started on his back. *Sowilo, uruz, ewhaz, gebo.* My hand was aching and, not for the first time, I wished that I was completely ambidextrous.

When the last rune was done, Kass and I put down our paintbrushes and held hands over Benji's prone form. This was the tricky bit. We both called our magic forward, until our hands started to glow. Then I pulled a little more from the depths of me, dredging up the last of it.

Our hands were now so bright that I couldn't look at them. It had to be enough because I didn't have any more to give. Our joined hands were trembling with the might of the magic pouring through us and if we didn't release it soon, it would burn us both out.

'On three,' I managed, my voice hoarse. 'One, two, three – *dagaz!*'

'Dagaz!' We intoned the word of power at the same time as we lowered our hands and touched them to Benji's chest. Deep inside his chest cavity, a jewel resided in lieu of a heart and the pulse of magic was acting as a defibrillator.

We watched his chest for signs of movement. This had to work because I didn't have it in me to raise that sort of power again. I was exhausted, on my feet through sheer stubbornness. Despair washed through me as his chest stayed stubbornly still and a sob escaped as I struggled to remain conscious. Oh, Goddess, don't take Benji from me.

As if she heard me, his chest rose. Relief swamped me, and I could do no more. 'Benji,' I murmured.

He was alive, but only time would tell if it was *my* Benji who had returned or just Benjamin Cohen. Whatever the outcome, I couldn't stay conscious a moment longer. I

swayed and let myself go. I felt arms catch me, and then I
knew no more.

Chapter 40

I awoke to the sounds of raised voices. Benji!

I sat bolt upright and looked around. I was alone in my room in The Witchery. A shard of panic pierced me. Where was Bastion? He'd been my shadow for days and now he was gone? I shoved off the covers impatiently. I was still dressed in my leggings and top.

I staggered as I took a few steps and hands from under my bed reached out and stabilised me. Panic thundered through me but, before I had a chance to react, the owner of the hands spoke. 'Easy, Bambi,' Bastion murmured.

Now that I'd found my footing, he released his hold and a moment later rolled out from under the bed. He did a neat flip thing and stood upright. He moved closer so there were only inches between us and his eyes swept over me. 'Are you all right, Amber?'

I stared at him, momentarily unable to do or say any-thing. He had been resting under my bed again, sleeping on the hard wooden floor so that I'd feel safe. My heart felt full to bursting.

The moment between us hummed with tension as I flicked my eyes to his lips and then licked my own. I was about to say something – I don't know what – but the shouting in the hallway was getting louder so I grimaced instead. I stepped back and slipped on my shoes.

'I'm okay, Griffin,' I teased. 'Let's see what this hulla-baloo is about.' Bastion sighed a little at the nickname. Maybe he'd think twice about calling Fehu 'Raven' now.

I recognised Oscar's angry voice in the cacophony out-side and I thought I heard Tristan's too. What the heck was Oscar doing arguing with a Council member? I opened the door, fixing for a fight with whoever had ruined that moment between Bastion and me. 'Enough!' I shouted as I went into the corridor. 'What's going on?' I put my hands on my hips. 'What a ruckus! You – speak.' I pointed at Tristan Farhand.

He frowned at being ordered around by a lowly witch when he was on the coven Council, but he deigned to speak. 'You have been summoned to the Council to ex-plain the recent events. These *gentlemen*,' he pointed at

Shirdal and Oscar, his tone indicating that he thought they were anything but gentlemen, 'refused to wake you. You have been summoned. Now!'

'I didn't think Council members delivered summons personally,' I noted caustically.

'We don't,' he snarled. 'But when one of us is dead, we do. You are to come with us, *now!*'

I realised what had put Oscar and Shirdal's backs up: Tristan's wizard bodyguard Mack was standing behind him, looking threatening and holding a pair of magic-cancelling cuffs. Bastion gave a low threatening growl when he saw them.

'Those won't be necessary,' I said firmly. 'I'll come now. Let's go.' Before they had a chance to even try and cuff me, I strode past them and down the stairs. Bastion kept pace with me, leaving Tristan and his guard almost trotting to keep up.

As we approached the coven chambers, I almost stumbled. There, on the door, was Benji. 'Benji?' I asked tremulously.

He beamed at me. 'Am!'

Thank the Goddess! I threw myself into his hard arms and hugged him for so long that the chill from his glacial skin leached into mine. Finally I drew back. 'You're okay?'

'I'm fine,' he reassured me. 'I felt bad about attacking Bastion, but he said it was all right. I still felt bad, but he said friends forgive each other. That's right, isn't it?' He searched my eyes for the truth.

I nodded decisively. 'Absolutely right. But Benji, there was nothing to forgive. It wasn't your fault, it was Hilary's.'

'I know, but I couldn't control myself.' His eyes dimmed. 'I would have felt very bad if I had hurt Bastion.'

'I know, but you didn't. He's right as rain. Benji – I'm so sorry I had to deactivate you.'

'That's okay, Amber DeLea. You had to save Bastion.' His tone was matter of fact, like I'd had no option, but he was wrong. I had saved Bastion through choice and, in doing so, I'd risked Benji. The fact that Benji was fine now was little consolation.

'I'm still very, very sorry.'

'As am I,' Benji admitted. 'I believe this feeling is remorse. I do not much like it, it makes my heart prickle. Shall we feel something else?'

I smiled. 'Let's. Let's feel happy that we're alive.'

Benji smiled. 'I *am* pleased about that. Thank you for reanimating me, Am.'

I kissed his cheek. 'You're so welcome.'

He cuddled me again briefly and whispered 'Am Bam' in my ear, which made me smile. Then his eyes flashed white. 'The Council will see you now,' he intoned formally. He opened the doors and once more I went into the witches' cauldron.

Chapter 41

The members were in full intimidation mode. The solitary 'guest' chair had been removed, and the spotlights turned to shine in my eyes. The remaining Council members were there with their cowls drawn up, and the central chair I had coveted for so long had been filled. Kass was sitting there, her cowl drawn up like the others, but I knew I had a friend and that steadied me.

'Describe the events that led up to Hilary's death,' Jasper's posh voice snapped.

Calmly and clinically, I explained what had first roused my suspicions about Hilary and went from there. I confirmed that she'd been listed by one of my potion-ingredient suppliers as having regularly purchased felfa. Murmurs went around the Council at that.

Arthur Starlin cleared his throat. 'We all know that felfa is used for more than black mordis.'

'Indeed we do,' I conceded. 'But that's not all.' I told them about Ria and the grim death of Meredith's familiar, Cindy; about Ria's suicide attempt and her remorse about the path she had started to take. 'She is hidden with her mother somewhere safe for now. But as she lay dying, she told us that the black coven does exist. Its members live among us.' I paused. 'Even here – I do not believe that Hilary was operating alone. You've started to wear your cowls all the time when you are meeting. Why?'

'Tradition,' sneered Tristan.

'Or,' I countered, 'to hide someone who isn't a coven Council member. If you are who you say are you, take down your cowls. You have nothing to hide.'

Kassandra did it straight away, revealing her long, warm-brown hair. Willow followed, her blonde tresses tumbling down, and looked around accusingly. 'If y'all are keeping your cowls up, you're hiding something. And I intend to find out what it is.'

With a huff, Carl Greenwood revealed his white beard, a pair of wire-rimmed glasses and a scowl. He reminded me of a crotchety Santa Claus.

There was the sound of a chair being scraped back and a clatter as it hit the floor. Someone – Seren, I think – cried out, 'Hey! You pushed me!' but I couldn't see what was going on because of the blinding spotlights.

'Bomb!' Bastion shouted in warning. He ran to me, shifting as he moved, and enveloped me in his wings as the bottle containing the potion bomb broke. The resulting boom was deafening inside the chamber and it made my ears ring. Purple witch fire burned and a choking smoke filled the room. The ceiling already had cracks in it and chunks of plaster rained down on us.

Then the screaming started.

Benji ran in. He slammed the door open, which gave the smoke somewhere else to go but also gave the purple flames more oxygen. Soon they'd burn out – witch fire burns hot and then it dies. Benji ghosted around the flames, reached up to the ceiling and his hands disappeared into it. He fought to stabilise it while the Council members were all blinking in confusion. Some were crying.

My ears were ringing. 'Is anyone hurt?' I shouted far too loudly. People were standing, brushing themselves off and removing their cowls. I recognised Arthur Starling, Tristan Farhand, Carl Greenwood, Jasper Ravenscroft, Willow Blackthorne, Seren Songbird, Isadora Grimshank, Rosalind Wilde and Octavia Ashby.

'I'm burnt,' Arthur said, 'but it'll keep.'

'I'm burnt, too,' Isadora said tremulously. 'Goddess, it hurts.' Willow ran to her and peeled back her cloak.

'She needs a burn salve!' Willow pronounced. 'It's bad.'

The room descended into chaos. There was so much shouting, and the smoke was making it hard to see what the hell was going on. I looked around, cataloguing the occupants. 'Where's Beatrice?' I yelled. 'And Felix?'

'Beatrice is here!' Carl shouted, 'She's on the floor, but she's hurt! She's alive but I don't know how long for. There's a lot of blood.'

Carl was an excellent potioneer but he wasn't so good at runes, especially when he was panicking. 'Someone get me a healing potion!' I ran to Beatrice and fell on my knees beside her.

She was unconscious. I checked her pulse; she was alive but she looked far too pale. 'Get me a brain-swelling reducer potion, too!' She'd hit her head and a pool of blood was spreading around her.

Without the healing potions, I did the next best thing I could. I checked my hands for cuts and, finding none, dipped my finger into her blood and crudely scrawled some runes on her. I painted *isa* for stasis, *algiz* for protection and *sowilo* for health. That would give us some time.

The purple flames had finally died, leaving scorch marks on the floor. They had burned away the red carpet, exposing part of the pentagram that was usually hidden underneath it. The acrid smoke was clearing, but panic and fear still laced the room. I could hear shouting and accusations and I grimaced; now wasn't the time to point fingers. We needed to heal our wounded. Why was nobody getting me the bloody potions I needed?

'It was Felix!' Jasper shouted.

'It *wasn't* Felix,' I countered from my position on the floor. 'It was whoever had taken Felix's place. The question is who was it – and what has happened to the real Felix? Where are my damned potions?'

There was a flurry of activity but I ignored it because finally the potions arrived, carried by a wide-eyed acolyte. Oscar passed me a paintbrush and I started painting.

Chapter 42

I was back in my room at the Witchery and exhaustion was crushing me. All the magic I'd used to reanimate Benji had really taken it out of me. Oscar had slipped me yet another vial of my ORAL potion when he noticed me scratching my arm. Next time I got the itchies, I'd have to pop into the Common realm for a proper re-charge.

My ORAL potion had been carefully distributed amongst the covens. Somewhat unfairly, the most powerful witches had been allocated individual vials so they could put more time in for their coven. It made sense: they could charge at higher rates than the acolytes or new witches, and time is money. I'd need to brew some more ORAL, but first we needed Lucy to sort out the small matter of the supply of kelpie water.

I took out my phone and logged in remotely to the coven's system. I checked the roster was up to date and skimmed the emails into which I'd been cc'd. 'What are you doing?' Bastion asked.

He'd made me jump. 'Oh! Just checking on the coven. Making sure everything is okay at home.' There was a message from Willow that made me frown. 'Damn it.'

'What?'

'Hilary's house has been broken into and torn apart. If there was any evidence of foul play, it was destroyed before the coven enforcers got to it. No black artefacts, nothing. Damn it,' I repeated.

That made it far more likely that there would be a formal investigation into her death. Oscar's footage hadn't been as clear as I'd hoped, and the section where she'd confessed to killing Abigay was somewhat muffled. Hopefully a tech guy could clean it up. I'd killed Hilary to defend Bastion; although no one had said anything, I'd been banking on Hilary's house being crammed to the rafters with manacles, blades and bloodwork bowls.

Bastion was studying me. 'What does it mean for you?'

'It means that, if we're trying to hunt down the whole blooming black coven, it's going to be that much harder. We were too slow to react and they swept in and destroyed everything. The business with the fake Felix threw us all. The footage has suddenly become very important.' I bit my nail. 'If we can't clean this up, there's a real risk I'll be charged with her death.'

'That's absurd,' Bastion growled. 'We can all give evidence to clear your name.'

'I didn't say I'd go down for it, but I could be arrested.' I grimaced. 'Wouldn't that be a proud day for Mum?'

Oscar shook his head. 'She'd know you did the right thing.'

'On a good day,' I whispered.

Bastion stood. 'I know a tech guy. If it's urgent, I can sort the footage. Now.'

I was so damned tired and so grateful that my eyes filled with tears but I didn't let them fall. 'Could you?'

He nodded briskly. 'He'll take some persuading and I'll need to do it in person. Give me the phone. I'll sort this,' he promised. He looked at me and hesitated. He didn't want to leave me.

'We've just struck a blow to the black coven. I'll be safe while they're licking their wounds. Go – I'll be fine. It'll only be a few hours.'

'Shirdal has gone to check on your mum. You only have Oscar.'

'Oscar has kept me alive for most of my life. Go. Sort the footage. Please, Bastion.'

It was the last sentence that did it. His eyes flared with something hot that made my stomach lurch. He held my gaze for a long moment before fixing Oscar with a different type of stare. 'You keep her safe while I'm away.' It wasn't a question but an order.

'Of course.' Oscar nodded. If he was affronted at Bastion's vehemence, he didn't show it.

Bastion saw himself out and I watched him leave. I still hadn't had a moment to tell him how I felt, and time was pressing on. I remembered his body, pale and unmoving, and I swallowed. I'd find the time.

I felt more nervous than I'd expected when Bastion had gone. Surely I'd be fine? Krieg had pulled his ogres off the contract that was out on me, and the black witches were reeling.

I tried to lose myself in more coven paperwork. We had managed to find two black witches, Ria and Hilary. Maybe I wasn't as bad at this detective stuff as I feared.

My shoulders slumped. Goddess knew how many other black witches there were out there in the black coven. We seemed to have reached boiling point; keeping off the radar was no longer on the black coven's agenda and that changed everything.

For the worse.

Chapter 43

There was a knock at the door. 'It's Kass. I've got a cup of bedtime tea, if you have a minute.'

If ever there were words that would force me to open my door, it was those. I rose and let her in. Becky followed her in carrying a silver tray with four porcelain cups and a pot of tea. There were no biscuits – who serves tea without a biscuit or a cake? A total animal, that's who.

'Shall I...?' Becky offered.

Kass smiled at her PA. 'Honestly, you've been run off your feet all day. If you hadn't insisted that you'd drive me home to Liverpool later, I would have let you go.'

'I like helping you.' Becky smiled at her.

'I know you do, but I'll pour the tea. You sit.'

Sitting space was limited so Becky hopped on the edge of the bed and Oscar leaned against the wall. Kass and I sat at the little table in the corner of the room.

'Milk? Sugar?' Kass asked.

We murmured our preferences and she poured the tea and handed out the cups. I closed my eyes as I sipped; I was so tired and thirsty that it barely touched the sides, and I guzzled the hot liquid down in seconds.

'Can Amber and I have a minute?' Kass asked Oscar and Becky.

'Sure.' Becky hopped off the bed, carefully balancing her full cup.

Oscar looked at me and I nodded. 'I'll be outside the door if you need me,' he promised.

I nodded again. Bastion should be back soon; I couldn't imagine fiddling with a phone would take *that* long, unless his tech guy was in London or something.

I had a pretty good idea what Kass wanted to talk about because if we were to continue our friendship there was something we needed to discuss. We couldn't leave it like a phoenix in the room.

The door shut. Kass fiddled uncomfortably with the tea set.

'We're friends, right?' I said. She nodded. 'So spit it out.'

She gave a rueful smile. 'This job should have been yours. If you hadn't left during testing...'

'But I did, and I chose to leave knowing full well what it would mean,' I said brusquely. Shoulda, woulda, coulda helped no one, as Abigay had pointed out.

'In the whole Felixgate mess, you kept your cool,' Kass sighed. 'You were throwing out orders like a drill sergeant.'

I grinned. 'I was made to rule. But maybe ruling my coven is enough.'

Kass shook her head. 'You were better during the emergency than I was.'

'To be fair, Kass, I can't tell you how many emergencies I've dealt with lately. I've become a little inured to danger – and I don't think that's a good thing. As I said, I left the test. I chose Oscar over the job. Maybe the coven Council deserve someone who will put the position above everything else.'

Kass snorted. 'If one of my parents had been in danger, you bet your ass I would have put them first. Family first, always.'

I didn't disagree. Suddenly my head started swimming. I blinked several times but it didn't clear. I reached a hand up to my head. 'Kass... I feel funny.' My ears were ringing with a sound that was blaring on and off.

She frowned at me. 'Are you tired?'

COVEN OF THE WITCH

'Something else.' My words were slurring – I'd drunk that damned tea too quickly. I'd been so thirsty that I hadn't paid attention to the little voice that had said it tasted a bit off. 'Poison,' I muttered.

Kass's eyes widened in panic. She grabbed my cup, pulled my hand to her and painted *isa* on me with the remaining tea. Stasis: it would be weak because of the lack of a potion, but she funnelled enough power into it for it to do its thing.

My head was still swimming. I blinked and suddenly Kass was helping me onto the floor and laying me in the recovery position. 'I'll get a potion!' she promised urgent-ly.

The door opened. 'Becky! Thank goodness! Amber's been poisoned! Have you got any potions on you?'

'Yes.' Becky smiled. 'But none that will help you.'

Kass frowned in confusion, then raised a hand to her head. 'Oh no. I don't feel so good either.' She slid boneless-ly into a chair and groaned. I could feel her pain as I hung on to consciousness through sheer force of will. Luckily, I am the stubbornest witch around.

'Finally,' Becky harrumphed. 'Oscar downed his tea and was out like a light more than a minute ago.' She peered into Kass's cup. 'You didn't drink it all yet, that's why. Who sips tea?' she muttered to herself. She looked at me. 'Is she dead?' she asked Kass, kicking me for good measure. The *isa* was keeping my muscles in stasis so I didn't move.

Becky laughed and clapped her hands. 'Well *finally!* I've been trying to kill that bitch for ages. I was really pissed off when she didn't explode into smithereens – and don't even get me started on the ogres' incompetence.'

Kass was blinking at Becky in shock. 'We weren't even at the coven when Amber's room was bombed.' Her words were slow; she was finding it difficult to think.

'*You* weren't at the coven. You had dinner with your friends and I said I had a headache and wanted an early night, remember? I had Ria paint a rune on Ada Marlowe's brat – she was supposed to kill him but she was too weak willed. She made him take a nap and hid him instead. And while DeLea was occupied, I slid into her home and rigged the bedroom to blow up. I was so excited about it.' She stamped her foot petulantly. 'She was supposed to *die.*'

She knelt down and looked at my unblinking eyes. My chest was barely moving and my heart was beating sluggishly. 'She doesn't even look like him,' Becky snarled as she studied me. 'She has his eyes and that's it.'

'Who?' Kass murmured weakly. I could see out of the corner of her eye that she was trying to draw her backpack towards her with her feet. I hoped she had a weapon in there – at that point even a potion bomb would have been welcome. I was dying – I could feel it. At least with a potion bomb, we could take this bitch with us.

'Daddy, of course. DeLea is my half-sister. Can't you see the family resemblance?' Becky mocked. 'And yet, she's Daddy's favourite. "Don't kill your sister! If you hire more ogres I'll disown you." *I'm* the black witch! Me! He was fine with the Crone being slaughtered and she was *somebody* – but touch DeLea? Hell, no. It's outrageous. One rule for one and one rule for the other. *I'm* the black witch. *I* followed in his footsteps. *I'm* the one that deserves his damned attention!'

She sounded like a spoiled brat who clearly hadn't had enough hugs during her childhood. Mum had been a hard taskmaster, but she had loved me unreservedly and I'd known it every single day of my life.

I could feel myself drifting off and I let myself go. Weird: I'd never thought that I'd die before Mum. That wasn't the natural order of things, but I found I was rather happy at the thought. I couldn't have survived burying her. I hoped that Oscar would take care of her.

Oscar! The thought of him stirred my blood. He'd been poisoned, too! I couldn't give up, couldn't stop, not now.

With a supreme effort, I pulled myself back to the moment. My apparent half-sister was still yattering on, enjoying her villain's monologue. I'd never had a sister and I'd always wondered what it would be like to be raised in a multi-children household. It turned out I wasn't someone who got on with their siblings.

I fought against the weak *isa* Kass had scrawled on me and felt it give a little, enough to unlock my right hand so I could reach into my pocket and pull out the potion bomb. *Sorry, Kass,* I thought dully as I groggily pulled my lethargic magic towards me then pushed it out towards the potion bomb.

The bomb dropped from my numb, unresponsive hand and rolled across the floor towards Becky. I was weak and I'd barely managed to propel it at all, so it moved achingly slowly. *Too close to me*, I thought dully, but the explosion would bring people running. People who could save Kass and Oscar. And that was okay.

I was glad Bastion was safe.

The bomb exploded.

Chapter 44

It was the beeping that woke me. My eyes fluttered open. 'Well,' the Scottish nurse said, with a smile, 'you're a stubborn one.'

I smiled faintly. That was an understatement; I invented stubborn.

'You're at the Royal Infirmary of Edinburgh in the cross-over ward.' A cross-over ward is warded against any Common realm intrusions, and every patient – and doctor and nurse – is Other. The witch in front of me was also a fully-qualified human nurse.

I looked around and my eyes settled on Bastion. He was in a chair beside my bed; his head slumped uncomfortably on his chest.

'You were dying, hen,' the witch said, her tone matter of fact. 'You were covered in third-degree burns and the poison was shutting down your internal organs, even with the *isa* that Member Scholes painted on you. Then this braw man appeared by your side,' she pointed to Bastion, 'and he did something. Nae idea what, but we're here now. We healed you of the burns and started to try and heal the internal damage but it was already done. He's no' moved since.'

I made a noise of distress and tried to push myself up. 'Sorry,' the nurse said. 'I didn't mean to worry ye. He's fine. I've checked his vitals. He's breathing, he's healthy, he's just scunnered.'

'Scunnered?' I asked hoarsely.

'Tired, knackered, done in. Whatever you want to call it.' She helped me sit up and passed me some water to sip through a straw. 'Frankly, you're a miracle. The Goddess has blessed you.'

The Goddess – or Bastion. 'How are Oscar and Kassandra?' I asked urgently as my brain kicked in.

'Kassandra is in the bed over there. She wasn't as burnt as you, nor had she ingested as much poison, but she didn't have a miracle man turn up for her. She'll be fine but it'll take her a wee bit longer to recover. The stress has made her fibromyalgia flare up so she's been placed in a healing coma for now. She'll be out of it for a while.'

'And Oscar?'

'Och, he's fine. He received medical attention at the site of the explosion. Councillor Blackthorne saw to him.'

Willow. I sank back into my sheets. Thank the Goddess: Willow was a brilliant healer. 'Everyone's okay?'

'Well, the one died – Becky Chose – but we're supposing you did that on purpose.'

I nodded. 'She's the one that poisoned me.'

The nurse busied herself tidying up around me. 'The Connection will want to speak to you, though Councillor Blackthorne is making lots of noise about them overstepping their authority. This is a coven matter. If they try to see you, I'll wake you and give you a head-start, hen.'

I smiled; I was beginning to like her. When she made me tea and toast, I gratefully ate the toast but I stuck to water; it was entirely too soon for me to drink tea. If Becky had ruined tea for me forever, I'd never forgive her. But then she was already dead, killed by a potion bomb rolled over by my own fair hands.

I sipped my water and closed my eyes. I'd killed my own sister – so much for families first. I guessed I should tweak that phrase to 'non-murdering families first'. From what she'd said, my father hadn't been thrilled about her attempts to kill me. Was it nice that my black-witch father didn't want me dead? I felt weird about the whole thing.

Becky had talked about ogres, so maybe all the recent attempts on my life had been made by her, a jealous sibling. She'd glared at me from the moment we'd met, and she'd tried to kill me before that. I'd done nothing to incur her wrath but live. She wasn't rational; she was a psychopath.

I wondered how I would have turned out if I'd been raised by my black-witch father? I struggled with empathy at the best of times. What if I'd been raised to disregard it? To think emotions were weak? I already had problems accepting that I needed to cry...

Morality is something we are taught, not something inherent – or so it seemed to me. If I hadn't been taught that causing pain was wrong, would I have been like Becky?

'I can hear your thoughts from over here,' Bastion murmured.

'Bastion!' I flung the covers off and tried to walk to him. Naturally my legs gave way.

He caught me before I collapsed on the floor. 'Whoa there, Bambi.' His arms were warm around me; his eyes were tired but he was incredibly close.

'That's the second time you've called me that,' I noted inanely.

'Do you not like it?' he asked softly.

'I don't know. I haven't had a proper nickname before. It's kind of nice. Bambi was a boy deer, though.'

'He was, but he suffered great adversity and grew into an excellent leader who spent his life helping others. It fits.'

I was speechless. 'You think that of me?'

His lips turned up the faintest amount and his dark eyes warmed. 'I do.'

I let myself go. Perhaps it had been all the introspection about Becky, but I let myself move and buried my head in the crook of his shoulder so he wouldn't see me cry. I'm not a dainty crier with a solitary tear rolling down my pale skin; nope, I snot and sob and my skin goes bright red. But I let myself cry. That was growth, for me.

When the tears finally stopped, I took a long breath. 'I'm only emotional because of the nearly dying thing.'

'Amber, you don't need to be embarrassed. You've been through a lot – a helluva lot. You are wholly justified in needing time to process that. If you weren't crying, there'd be something wrong with you.'

Like something had been wrong with Becky.

I pulled back a little so I could see his face, but not enough to climb out of his lap. 'Can you get me out of here?' I asked abruptly, then gave a head thunk. 'Of course you can't. You were passed out a moment ago.'

'I didn't pass out. I was in a regenerative coma,' he corrected.

'What's the difference?'

He grinned. 'Mine sounds intentional.'

'Was it?'

'Not especially, no.' That surprised a laugh out of me. 'I'm fine now, back to full strength.'

'You can't possibly be!'

'Remember how quickly I recovered from the black witch's curse way back at the start of my bodyguard detail?'

I nodded.

'I've always been a man that recovers fast.' He gave me a quick wink, so I would know that he was flirting with me, and I was strangely pleased to hear some innuendo from him. Life had been so insane the last few days that I needed a bit of harmless flirting if only to reassure myself that my feelings weren't totally one sided.

As if to prove how strong he was, he stood up with me cradled in his arms then shifted me around so he was holding my entire weight with one arm. He flicked through the charts and doctor's notes hooked over the end of the bed and gave a nod of satisfaction. 'You'll be all good with some R&R. Let's get you out of here.'

'What about Kass?' I said. 'She's still out.'

'Shirdal's here. He'll keep an eye on her until she's okay.'

'He's here? Wasn't he with my mum?'

'Bambi, you've been out of it for two days.'

'Goddess. And you? How long have you been out of it?'

'A day. I'm fine. You're fine.'

Tension drained from my shoulders. He was right; it had been touch and go but we were both okay. I wrapped my hands more firmly around his neck. 'You're right. Get us the hell out of here.'

'As you wish.'

Chapter 45

Bastion set me down so that I could totter to Oscar under my own steam.

Oscar pushed off the car as soon as he saw me. 'Amber!' He ran to me, threw his arms around me and kissed me fiercely on the forehead. 'Oh my God, kid, you scared me so badly. Are you okay?' He drew back to examine me.

'I'm okay – a little flimsy. I just need food and rest.'

'What food do you want? I'll buy it all.'

I laughed a little. 'I'm okay, Oscar.'

'No thanks to me!' His voice was dark and bitter, full of self-recrimination.

'Hey!' I said sharply, wagging a finger at him. 'You were poisoned, too! I don't blame you in the slightest, and you shouldn't blame yourself either. Bastion, tell him!'

There was a beat of silence that went on a fraction too long. 'We blame Becky,' Bastion said finally. 'Each of us

COVEN OF THE WITCH

is only responsible for our *own* actions. We can't control what others do. She was the one who poisoned you two and that wasn't your fault. It was Becky's. And she paid for it.'

'Are we okay?' I asked Oscar. 'I don't think I can cope if we're not.'

'Of course we are. I feel like I let you down, but that's a "me" issue and I'll work through it. But bear with me for a couple of weeks while I smother you, okay?'

I grimaced; I hate being smothered. 'Thirty minutes of smothering per day for three weeks, and then we're business as usual. Deal?'

Oscar laughed. 'Deal. Get in the car. We should probably roll.'

Bastion flashed Oscar a grin. 'Did you do it?'

'Yup.'

'Do what?' I asked.

'Get in the car and see.'

I slid into the car, buckled on my seatbelt – safety first – and gaped as I saw Benji sitting in the front seat. 'Benji!'

He was wearing sunglasses and a suit jacket; he looked like he was auditioning for a role in *Men in Black*. He flashed me a grin. 'Am Bam! I'm so happy to see you looking so much better.' Oscar had the radio on, and Benji was nodding his head in time to Nirvana. I never would have pegged the golem for a rocker.

Bastion slid in next to me as Oscar started the engine. 'We need to hustle,' he said.

'What's the hurry?' I asked.

'Technically we don't have permission to take Benji.'

'We're stealing him?' A smile tugged at my lips.

'Better to ask for forgiveness than permission,' Bastion said sanctimoniously then ruined the effect by winking.

I snorted. 'I think we have a thievery problem – first the CD and then this!' I paled. 'Oh my God. The CD...'

Bastion reached over squeezed my hand. 'It was in our bedroom at The Witchery.'

Oscar cleared his throat. 'We looked through the rubble – but we couldn't find it.'

All of that information on my father ... gone. Rune ruin!

Chapter 46

I snoozed on the drive home and barely woke as Bastion lifted me out of the car and carried me up the coven stairs. He murmured good night to Oscar. Benji peeled off to sleep on Oscar's sofa; I'd offered him the use of the top floor, but I think he liked the novelty of having a roommate. Oscar also seemed more than happy to have company after all he'd been through. They were talking about rock music as they walked away.

By the time we reached my room, I was more awake. The power of a good nap.

'Cup of tea?' Bastion asked.

I shook my head vehemently. 'Not now – maybe not ever.'

'You can't let them take away the things you love.'

'Easier said than done.'

He studied me. 'A hot chocolate or a chamomile infusion?'

'A hot chocolate would be great. Please.'

I slumped onto my sofa and watched the gorgeous man as he effortlessly moved around my kitchen caring for me. Then my wards flared and my heart stopped for a moment. I sent out my magic – and the feeling was distinctly griffinish. I'd felt it before and now it made sense. It was Fehu; linked as he was to Bastion, he gave off a griffinish vibe.

I rose to let him in through my balcony door. He flew in and circled the room before settling on my shoulder and chittering intensely at me. He was telling me off.

'He's mad at you for getting hurt,' Bastion said over the sound of the kettle.

'Well, tell him it wasn't my fault,' I huffed.

'It doesn't matter. Just let him get it out of his system.' He grinned ruefully. 'He likes you.'

The raven continued to kraa and clack at me as I reached up and stroked his soft feathers. 'I'm happy to see you, too. I'm glad you're okay.'

Fehu huffed; there was no other word for it. I continued to stroke him and finally he fell silent and started weaving my loose hair into some sort of nest. I left him to it. I'd brush it out eventually and it seemed to calm him.

Bastion sat next to me and handed me my hot chocolate. It had whipped cream with a chocolate flake sticking out of the top, my favourite type, crumbly and delicious. He'd found my emergency stash in the kitchen drawer.

'Wow. You can come again,' I joked. I set the drink down on the table and turned to face him. Whatever it was between us – this thing – it was burning me up. The tension, the heat, was killing me. Life was too short and it was time to do something about it.

I was going to kiss him.

I moved a little closer and Bastion met my eyes, but he wasn't smouldering like I'd expected. Instead he looked nervous. 'Amber,' he cleared his throat. 'We need to talk.'

No good conversation ever followed those words.

Chapter 47

'We need to talk about Jake,' Bastion continued regret-fully.

'No, we don't,' I blurted in panic. I didn't want to talk about Jake. I was finally moving on, even if only a little, and bringing him up now seemed cruel when I was inches away from the first kiss I'd had in years.

Bastion moved further away and I sighed, closed my eyes and let my head drop in defeat. 'Please,' Bastion murmured. It was the first 'please' I could recall him saying and it made me freeze. I wanted to hear that word fall from his lips again, but in very different circum-stances. I swallowed hard.

Bastion tugged me over to a dining-room chair to put some space between us. 'Sit,' he ordered though his tone was gentle. I expected him to take the other chair but instead he knelt in front of me like a sinner begging for forgiveness.

What more could he tell me about Jake? What could be worse than having caused his death? Something dark and panicky churned in my gut. I didn't want to hear it, whatever it was. I braced myself and met his eyes. 'Go on then. Say your piece.

Bastion licked his lips. 'I didn't kill Jake.'

I stared at him. Whatever I'd been expecting, it hadn't been that. 'What?' I said finally, when my brain started firing again. 'But you told Jinx you had.' And Jinx is a truth-seeker, she can tell when you lie. Always.

He shook his head. 'No. I told Jinx I'd coaxed him.'

'What's the difference? You coaxed him to kill himself.'

'That's what I implied to Jinx, but although I coaxed Jake it wasn't to make him kill himself,' he confessed. 'I coaxed him to talk to me.'

'I don't understand,' I said blankly. My heart was hammering.

'I showed up at his door and he was expecting me – well, not me but an assassin. It turned out that removing his eyesight had gifted him with a touch of the sight.'

'He knew he was going to die,' I said dully.

'He knew that various paths were stretching ahead of him and in all of them he would die. He'd come to terms with it. He said that the path that would be best for you was for him to kill himself. I asked him to tell me more but he refused, so I coaxed him to sit down and talk. We had a cup of tea and we talked about the different ways his life could end.'

Bastion licked his lips again. 'The best route was for him to kill himself and me to take the blame. I could continue working for the Connection, and using its links would enable me to help more people. Help you. Like with the phone footage.'

'You didn't kill Jake?' I repeated blankly.

'No,' he confirmed. 'He was ready to die. He faced it like a warrior.'

'He jumped off of the roof.' My voice broke.

Bastion's eyes were sympathetic. 'He did.'

'Of his own volition?' I asked again. To be clear, to be sure.

'Yes.'

My mind was whirring and my heart was aching. 'All of this time you let me hate you for something you didn't do. Why?'

'Death is hard and you needed someone to blame.' He shrugged like it was no big deal.

'I nearly killed you because of it!' My voice started to rise hysterically. 'I nearly let the black witch's curse kill you for something you didn't do! Fucking hell, Bastion! You let everyone believe you'd killed him, even Jinx.'

He grimaced a little. 'It was a hard one for Jessica Sharp to reconcile with her affection for me, but I believe she has forgiven me.'

'But there's nothing to forgive.'

'No, and if you're okay with it I'd like to tell her that one day. She blames herself for leading the Connection to the property and for all that followed.'

'Of course you must tell her the truth,' I said automatically.

My mind was lost and silence reigned for five long minutes. Bastion was still kneeling before me, looking at me with concern. 'Amber, are you okay?'

'It's a lot,' I said finally. 'He really did kill himself.'

'Not to leave you, not to hurt you. The Goddess told him it had to be.'

I scrubbed eyes that were suddenly hot and full. 'This is why I hate prophecy,' I muttered. 'Fucking future. You have to be so careful with it. The wrong word here or there, and you can change everything. It's such a responsibility. Hearing the Goddess and being guided by the stars weighed on Abigay. And Mum keeps mentioning prophecy. I've been avoiding it because I despise it, but it keeps coming for me time and time again.'

My voice was bitter. 'My poor Jake.' Tears fell then at the thought that he'd stared into his own future and seen nothing but a hundred deaths. No kids for us, no chance of them, not then, not ever. No chance of anything but a cold grave.

I wept for the future Jake and I could never have had, and Bastion held me while I cried.

Chapter 48

Sleep had been a long time coming and I'd needed a little space from Bastion while I processed all that he'd told me. He'd respected my boundaries and, although we'd shared a bed, he'd made sure he was as far away from me as possible.

I showered, runed and dressed. Brushing out the little nest Fehu had made in my hair took a while but I found it hard to be annoyed. He'd only done it because he'd been agitated and needed to calm down.

I stared into the mirror and said my affirmations. Every day I have a goal, something to achieve, but that day I felt numb. 'Today I will ... get through the day.' I nodded to myself. Sometimes that's enough.

A bowl of overnight oats was waiting on the dining room table with a glass of orange juice. 'Good morning, Bambi.' Bastion's voice was soft and unsure. I'd never heard that tone before.

The use of the nickname pulled a smile from me. 'Good morning, Bastion.'

He studied me as he so often did, taking in the circles under my eyes, then asked a superfluous question. 'Did you sleep okay?'

I grimaced. He knew that I hadn't. 'It took a while for my mind to stop whirring.'

'I'm sure. I'm sorry.'

'It's not your fault.' I paused. 'I'm glad you told me the truth, I really am. It's just brought up all that stuff again. Just ... give me a little time, okay?' I felt raw and exposed and I hoped he understood.

'As much time as you need.' He hesitated. 'May I have a hug?'

I blinked. Such a simple request. 'Of course.' I closed the distance between us and wrapped my arms around him. Instantly his scent settled around me and the tension drained from my body. His hard muscles were pressed against me and his arms warmed me.

I let a soft sigh slip out. Hugs with Bastion might be one of my new favourite things. He didn't seem to be in a hurry to release me, so I stayed there, nestled into him, enjoying his warmth.

Finally, as I reluctantly started to pull back, he gave me one last squeeze before releasing me. I realised that I didn't feel lonely. Often that feeling dogged me, no matter how much company I had, but at that moment it was gone. 'You give great hugs,' I murmured.

'I'm glad you enjoyed it. It made me feel better, too.'

'Me too. Let's do it again some time,' I suggested lightly.

'As often as you want.'

I cleared my throat and seized my courage. When Bastion had said 'we have to talk' the previous night, *this* was what I'd been envisaging. It was time for us to face the phoenix in the room.

'I haven't dated in forever – or ever, really – so I'm not very good at this. But I wanted to check that we're on the same page. It would be awkward if we weren't or if we weren't even reading the same book.' Damn it, I was rambling. *Just say it DeLea.* 'I like you, Bastion.' I felt myself flush and I fixed my eyes on his shoulder. 'Like *fancy you* like you.'

Oh my Goddess, was I twelve? This was mortifying. I closed my eyes and buried my head in my hands. I was *forty-two* and an accomplished and well-respected witch. And here I was, blushing over telling a boy that I liked him.

Bastion pulled my hands gently but firmly from my face and I looked up at him, expecting to see humour in his eyes. I was ready to be teased. But there was no humour; there was heat. They were bedroom eyes. 'I fancy you too, Amber DeLea.' His voice was husky.

'Really?' Thank the Goddess!

Now came the humour. His lips turned up. 'Is it so hard to believe?'

'Yes.'

'I don't buy romance books for just anyone, Amber.'

I smiled. 'One day, I want to go into a bookstore with you.'

'I thought we weren't ready to do dirty talk yet?'

A laugh burst out of my chest and he looked pleased with himself. 'Slow and steady, witch. We only get our first kiss once and I'm not in a hurry. Anticipation makes life all the more sweet.'

He stepped closer to me, meeting my eyes before looking down at my lips. He met my gaze again and his eyes were hot. My heart was thundering; whilst I absolutely appreciated his patience and lack of pressure, everything about him made me want to throw myself at him.

The tension hummed between us; we were so close that I fancied I could feel the heat from his skin. Our lips were barely an inch apart, his breath was ghosting across my skin ... and then he stepped back.

He sat at the dining table and dug into his morning oats.

Bloody hell. My heart was hammering and my tummy was twisting deliciously. 'Tease,' I accused him.

He looked up from his oats. His eyes were still intense; he wasn't as calm as I'd thought. He wasn't unaffected. 'Yes,' he said simply. 'I do like teasing. When you're ready – when *we're* ready – there's going to be a whole lot of begging.' He smiled ruefully. 'And in the meantime, I am just going to be sacrificing a whole bunch of future heirs in your name.'

Another laugh burst from me. 'Poor heirs.' I blushed at the thought of him sacrificing heirs alone, in the shower, maybe. I bit my lip.

'You're worth it.' Bastion winked then the humour left his face. 'Now come and eat breakfast. You can't run on empty. Plus Oscar's put some kind of cinnamon and apple yoghurt in the oats. They're delicious.'

I dug in; he was right, they *were* delicious, but I still couldn't get rid of the idea of Bastion spilling his seed into his hands while he thought of me. Eventually I dragged my filthy mind to something else. Thoughts of his hypothetical heirs eventually made me think of his real heir, his daughter Charlize.

'I need to see my mum,' I said abruptly when my bowl was empty.

Bastion didn't blink at the change in gears. 'No problem, I assumed you would. I'll let Charlize and Haiku know to expect us.'

'Thanks.' I texted Oscar about my plans and got a positive response. We'd meet by the car in thirty minutes.

I couldn't wait to get to my mother. I needed to see that she was okay with my own eyes.

Chapter 49

They had stashed Mum away in a little suburban house in Beaconsfield. The village was a mixture of red-brick houses and white-rendered ones slashed with dark wooden beams, Tudor style. Mum was in one of the white ones. The garden was neat and tidy; I would never have guessed in a million years that it was a griffin safe house. I guessed that was the point.

Benji was looking around at the village in wonder.

'You okay Benji?'

'I've never been out of Edinburgh,' he confessed. 'The drive home last night was in the dark so I couldn't see too much. Is everywhere so beautiful?'

'No,' I laughed. 'Beaconsfield is particularly beautiful. If we have time one day, I'll take you to the model village.' Bekonscot model village and railway is tiny and beautiful. The image of this huge golem lumbering amongst all the miniature artefacts made me smile. It was nice to imagine days out together. Most friends might prefer the pub but Benji would appreciate this more. We didn't need to do things like everyone else; we'd carve our own way.

'Come on, I want you to meet my mum.' I hesitated. 'She's got dementia – or something like it – so she doesn't always know what's going on. She has good days and bad ones.'

He touched my shoulder lightly. 'That must be hard for you, Am.'

'It is. She was a real force of nature – and she still can be! But it depends on the day and I'm not sure what all this upheaval will have done to her. Routine usually helps, so...' I trailed off.

Benji smiled. 'It will be my honour to meet her.'

Bastion took point and knocked on the oak door. Charlize opened it and nodded at him briskly then stepped back to let us in. She looked a little like her dad, with black hair, golden skin and big eyes. She was beautiful.

It suddenly occurred to me that I had no idea who *her* mum was or if she was even alive. The griffin population was dangerously low; it was estimated to be in double figures, forty or fifty worldwide, but the griffins were tight-lipped about it. Rumour said they hadn't had new chicks for a century, but Charlize didn't *look* old. Then again, neither did Bastion and I knew he was more than two hundred years old. I should talk to Bastion about these things.

Charlize nodded politely. 'Luna is through here. Follow me.'

Mum was in the conservatory. There were paintbrushes and paint and canvasses as far as my eyes could see. My heart swelled; they were taking good care of her. 'Thank you so much,' I murmured to Charlize.

'She loves painting. It keeps her stable.' Did I detect a hint of affection in her tone?

I nodded. 'She's always been happiest with a paintbrush in her hand.'

'Don't talk about me as if I'm not here!' Mum sighed. 'Hello, Amber. You've come and you've brought guests. A golem! Outside Edinburgh! Now I've seen it all. My friend Abigay lives in Edinburgh, you should seek her out.'

My stomach dropped – she didn't remember that Abigay was dead. I struggled to clear the rock from my throat. 'This is Benji, a friend of mine,' I blurted instead.

'My honour to meet you, Benji.' Mum touched her hand to her heart and gave a little bow. Lucille was wrapped around her neck and gave a welcoming chitter.

'My honour to meet you, Mother of Amber.' Benji touched his hand to his heart and bowed deeply, a sign of great respect. He held the bow for twenty long seconds.

Mum gave a tinkling laugh. 'Up you get, Benji. That's enough respect for one day. And Mother of Amber is a bit of a mouthful. Luna, please! Of course I accomplished a great many things in my lifetime, besides giving birth to Amber.' She winked at me, teasing me. 'Though rearing her into the witch she's become remains one of my greatest achievements.'

Her eyes swept over Oscar with no recognition.

'My driver and Bastion,' I introduced them as colourlessly as possible.

'I know Bastion. You're looking well. As always.'

I wondered what age Mum thought I was, though it hardly mattered.

Charlize excused herself to go and patrol with the elusive Haiku, leaving us alone.

'Mum.' I hesitated, not quite sure how to broach the topic. 'We need to talk about my father. I – I got your CD from the deposit box in Liverpool, but it – it got destroyed. I'm so sorry.'

COVEN OF THE WITCH

She took in my anguished face. 'Gosh, no need to cry over spilt potions, Amber. It's okay, dear. Did you think I was foolish enough to keep only *one* copy?'

I had, actually. 'There's another?' I breathed, hope blooming in my chest.

'Of course. In my room. I hid it behind one of the paintings.' She frowned. 'I can't remember which one.' She looked around. 'I wasn't always here,' she muttered, suddenly looking small and frail and lost. My heart ached.

'You're just having a break, aren't you?' I kept my tone light.

She smiled. 'That's it. A little holiday, Charlize said.'

After her confusion, I kept the conversation as simple as I could. I mentioned nothing of the black coven or my near-death experience. 'A friend of mine was made the Symposium member,' I told her.

She smiled. 'Lovely,' she said vacantly. Suddenly, her eyes sharpened on my face. 'That was never supposed to be your destiny, Amber. When are you going to hear the prophecy?' She sounded exasperated. 'Abigay is dead. The time is nigh. Stop burying your head.'

I exchanged startled glances with Oscar at her sudden recollection of Abigay's passing. 'I found Abigay's killer,' I said it quickly, before the lucidity faded.

315

'Good.' Mum folded her arms. 'And were they punished?'

'Permanently,' I confirmed.

She looked at Bastion. 'At your hands?' Her tone was approving.

'At mine,' I interjected quietly.

Her eyes widened and she reached for my hand. 'Darling, I'm sorry. That must have been hard.'

Another day, the double standard would have made me snort – she was fine with Bastion killing them – but she was right. It *was* hard. It hadn't just been Bastion's confession about Jake keeping me awake last night. I'd *killed* my half-sister. It was a lot to deal with. 'Yes,' I said simply.

Mum raised my hand to her lips and kissed the back of it. 'You've got this, Amber. I believe in you every minute of every day.'

I nodded, a rock in my throat. She had done once, but now the minutes with me were few and far between.

'And Amber? When you find your father ... you'll need to be prepared to do the same again.'

I couldn't really remember him, but the thought of being responsible for my father's death made my gut churn. 'Is that what the Prophecy says?' I asked.

She grinned impishly. 'You'll have to get it and find out.'

'Why can't you just tell me?' I sighed.

'Some things you have to find for yourself. Plus, if I mis-remember a word or phrase, it could change its meaning. No, you must always hear a prophecy directly from the source.'

'The Hall of Prophecy.' I sighed.

'The seers,' she corrected. 'Melva, actually. Off you pop, Amber.' She waved me away.

I was dismissed.

Chapter 50

I reluctantly let Mum shoo us out after an hour. I'd stayed longer than usual and it was taxing for her, but I'd needed it so much. As we stood to leave, her gaze fixed on Oscar. 'Oz,' she called in wonder. He flew to her.

I gestured for the rest of us to leave to give them time to themselves. You had to make the most of the lucid moments and I wasn't in a hurry to leave, despite the huge to-do list that was weighing me down. I needed to formulate and brew a potion to find the ogre king's mate; I needed to find and listen to the damned prophecy; I needed to brew some more final defence potion for Bastion and Shirdal. And I needed to find that CD about my father. I'd settle for the latter as today's goal.

'Thank you,' I said to Charlize. 'You're clearly taking good care of her.'

'You're welcome. I owe you for your rescuing me, after all.' She slid a teasing glance to her father. 'Though I think Dad's eager to pay that tab for me.'

Without blinking he reached out and flicked her forehead, startling another laugh out of me. I hadn't laughed so much in years.

'You've been keeping up with your schedule?' Bastion asked his daughter quietly, searching her eyes.

'I have. I promise.'

It was hard to imagine that the quiet young woman in front of me had built up quite a violent reputation. I suppose with being the daughter of Bastion – the world's pre-eminent assassin – she'd had little choice.

Bastion nodded, taking her at her word, then looked around with a frown. 'Where's Haiku? I haven't seen him but I feel his presence. And Apollinaire's.'

'Haiku is hiding from you.' She grinned.

Bastion raised an eyebrow. 'Why?'

'He's scared of you.'

'What is he doing that risks my ire?'

'We're having sex. Lots of it.'

'Not while you're on watch!' Bastion sounded scandalised. It made me snort that that was his only objection.

'Of course not! What do you take me for? That's why Apollinaire is helping us.'

'Watching over my mum, right? Not having a three-some?' I clarified.

Charlize laughed. 'Watching over your mum,' she confirmed. Her face turned serious. 'She's been teaching Apo to paint. We wouldn't risk her, any of us. We've never had to *protect* someone before and we quite like it.'

Bastion nodded solemnly. 'It is nice, isn't it?'

'Yes! And we still get to kill things. Win-win!'

A smile pulled at Bastion's lips. 'Indeed.'

Oscar stepped out of the room looking baleful. 'She slipped back.'

'I'll go to her,' Charlize said. 'I'll give her a fresh canvas. I've promised I'll hang all the ones she's painted in the house. She's very dogmatic about where she wants them.'

'She knows her own mind,' Oscar said but then his smile faded because she didn't, not these days. I squeezed his arm. He tried to smile again but it was more of a grimace. Poor Oscar, poor Mum, poor me.

'She does,' I agreed.

I watched discreetly as Bastion kissed Charlize on the forehead and ruffled her hair. That made her eyes roll. Then I cleared my throat. 'We'd better go.'

'Make like a banana and split.' Charlize grinned at her father.

'Make like an orange and roll,' Bastion countered.

I smiled again. They had such an easy relationship and I envied them. Oscar slung an arm around my shoulders, reminding me that they weren't the only ones.

'Let's go to the care home,' Oscar said. 'We have a CD to find.'

Chapter 51

The matron looked somewhat dismayed to see me. Charming.

'I need to get some things from my mother's room,' I said calmly. 'We'll go by ourselves.'

'Fine,' she said tightly. 'Any idea when she'll be returning to us?'

I shook my head. 'Not until the danger has passed.'

'And how long will that be?' She eyed Benji.

'How long is a witch's broomstick?'

She pressed her lips together. 'It is not good for your mother to be carted around. She gets the best care *here*. Routine is important.'

'I'm aware of that,' I responded coolly. 'Thank you for your concern.' I moved away before I could say something catty, like her concern related to the home's pay cheque rather than Mum's welfare. The matron never seemed especially *caring*, though the rest of the staff were always wonderful.

Mum's room was clean but largely undisturbed. I waited until we were all inside before shutting the door. 'Gentlemen, let's check those paintings.' It felt rude and invasive to be rifling through my mum's things when she wasn't there, but we had her permission so I tried to set my uneasiness to one side.

My phone rang, startling me. *Kassandra Scholes*, the screen said. Thank goodness she was awake. I swiped to answer. 'DeLea.'

'Amber!'

It was good to hear her voice and I closed my eyes with relief. 'Kass. I am so sorry about the bomb.'

'Don't be.' She laughed. 'I had exactly the same idea. I had my bomb in my backpack and I was trying to drag it towards me.' She paused. 'Becky – I still can't believe it. I spent virtually every single waking hour with her for more than two years. It's... I can't believe it,' she repeated. 'I *trusted* her.'

'I'm sorry. It's all rather shocking.'

'It is. Hilary was bad enough – to think she killed Abigay...' She trailed off then cleared her throat. 'Actually, that's why I'm calling you. The coven Council is mounting an investigation into the whole mess and you'll be called back to Edinburgh to give evidence, probably in the next day or two. To save face, they're pretending that Benji is with you as part of your protection detail – but some of them are really pissed off that you sneaked away with him. When you return, be on your guard.'

So what was new? 'Thanks for the warning.'

'Sure – what are friends for? So, how are you doing?'

'What?'

'You asked me to call – you know, to talk. So that's what I'm doing. How are you, Amber?'

I'm not very good at small talk. 'I'm okay.' I hesitated, 'I saw my mum this morning.'

'That's lovely.'

'Yeah, it is. She has dementia.' I blurted it out. Mum's condition was something I'd always kept to myself, more because of fear for her safety than privacy issues. But Kass had stood with me against a black witch, and if she'd been a member of the black coven Becky wouldn't have poisoned her. If there was one witch I could trust, it was Kass.

'I'm sorry, that must be hard on you. You're an only child, aren't you?' she asked.

'Yeah. You?'

'I have a brother. We get on well. His wife is nice, too.'

'That must be...' I paused. 'I'm actually not very good at small talk.'

'You'll get used to it.' I heard the humour in her voice. 'If ever you're stuck, just comment on the weather. That always gets people going.'

'True.' The Brits could compose sonnets to their ever-varied weather.

'And if you want people to avoid you, make eye contact and smile aggressively. It makes them run away – well, it does in the UK. I haven't tried it in other countries. It's kind of fun.'

'If you want to compound it,' I suggested, 'you could add on a chirpy "Have a nice day!".'

'A step too far my friend.' We laughed. This was nice.

'Got it!' Oscar called from Mum's bedroom.

'I'd better go. Kass?'

'Yes?'

'Thanks so much for calling to chat. I'm so pleased to hear from you.'

'We'll speak soon, Amber. Take care of yourself.'

She rang off, and I found that I was smiling.

Chapter 52

Bastion and I ate a companionable late lunch together, and I tried to get my brain to stop. I stood at the sink washing up the dishes, but when they were dry I finally gave in and asked the question that was still bothering me. 'What did you do? At the hospital? To save me?' I put the towel over the oven door.

Bastion grimaced. 'I can't answer that,' he said tightly.

I put my hands on my hips. 'Can't or won't?'

'Can't. Your mother bound Oscar and I tightly.'

'What has my mum got to do with it?' I said, exasperated.

'Everything.' He let out a small breath, a sigh for him. 'I've given you all the clues I can,' he said unhappily. 'It's up to you to connect the dots.'

'I was always rubbish at dot-to-dot as a child.'

'I have faith in you. You'll work this out.'

'What if I don't?'

'You will,' he promised.

The flat was spotless and I was procrastinating. Oscar was showing Benji around the coven, and Bastion and I had the CD. I sighed. 'We should look at this.'

'We don't have to if you're not ready.' He was being kind, but I knew I *had* to be ready. We couldn't risk losing the CD, not again. I needed to open it and learn its secrets before something happened to it.

'We could always kiss instead,' I suggested, only half joking. At least that would be one less thing on my to-do list.

Bastion smiled. 'Don't tempt me.' He crossed the distance between us and looped his fingers through mine. 'Come on, Bambi. Let's be brave together.' He was right; I needed to face whatever was on that CD.

He gently tugged our joined hands and led me into my home office. He sat on my office chair, booted up my desktop computer then pulled me onto his lap. I tried to perch lightly so I didn't put my full weight on him. 'None of that,' he murmured, pulling me down properly.

'I'm heavy.'

'You're perfect.'

I snorted. 'Now I know you're addled. Must be the centuries weighing on your poor mind.'

'Tease me at your peril,' he warned, but his tone was light.

'Oh yeah?' I was a tad breathless, wondering what his revenge would be. I could definitely get behind some teasing.

His eyes were dark as he watched the thoughts that were no doubt dancing across my expressive face. He kissed me lightly on my neck and then groaned as I wiggled a little in his lap. 'Don't think I don't know exactly what you're doing, Amber DeLea.'

'And what's that?'

'Procrastinating.'

Bastion inserted the CD and the cursor whirred to let us know it was loading. When it was ready, Bastion clicked on the button to open it. We both stared at the screen.

'Oh heck,' I muttered, sliding my head down so it thunked on the desk.

'Yeah,' Bastion sighed.

We were screwed.

The End.

Never fear! Familiar of the Witch is coming soon! Don't forget to pre-order!

To tide you over, here is a free bonus scene from Hex of the Witch from Bastion's point of view! https://dl.bookfunnel.com/1iisvjzelp It's funny how much Amber misses...!

Other Works by Heather

The *Other Realm* series

Book .5 Glimmer of Dragons (a prequel story),

Book 1 Glimmer of The Other,

Book 2 Glimmer of Hope,

Book 2.5 Glimmer of Christmas (a Christmas tale),

Book 3 Glimmer of Death,

Book 4 Glimmer of Deception,

Book 5 Challenge of the Court,

Book 6 Betrayal of the Court; and

Book 7 Revival of the Court.

The *Other Wolf* Series

Book .5 Defender of The Pack(a prequel story),
    Book 1 Protection of the Pack,
    Book 2 Guardians of the Pack; and
    Book 3 Saviour of The Pack.

The *Other Witch* Series

Book .5 Rune of the Witch(a prequel story),
    Book 1 Hex of the Witch,
    Book 2 Coven of the Witch;,
    Book 3 Familiar of the Witch, and
    Book 4 Destiny of the Witch.

The *Portlock Paranormal Detective* Series with Jilleen Dolbeare

Book .5 The Vampire and the case of her Dastardly Death,
    Book 1 The Vampire and the case of the Wayward Werewolf,(coming March 2024)

About Heather

Heather is an urban fantasy writer and mum. She was born and raised near Windsor, which gave her the misguided impression that she was close to royalty in some way. She is not, though she once got a letter from Queen Elizabeth II's lady-in-waiting.

Heather went to university in Liverpool, where she took up skydiving and met her future husband. When she's not running around after her children, she's plotting her next book and daydreaming about vampires, dragons and kick-ass heroines.

Heather is a book lover who grew up reading Brian Jacques and Anne McCaffrey. She loves to travel and once spent a month in Thailand. She vows to return.

Heather also finds it amusing to write about herself in the third person.

Want to learn more about Heather? Subscribe to her newsletter for behind-the-scenes scoops, free bonus material and a cheeky peek into her world. Her subscribers will always get the heads up about the best deals on her books.

Subscribe to her Newsletter at her website www.heatherg harris.com/subscribe.

COVEN OF THE WITCH

Too impatient to wait for Heather's next book? Join her (very small!) army of supportive patrons at Patreon. Her patron's get exclusive sneak peeks and advance access to Heather's books before they're published!

Contact Info: www.heathergharris.com

Email: HeatherGHarrisAuthor@gmail.com

Reviews

Reviews feed Heather's soul. She'd really appreciate it if you could take a few moments to review her books on Amazon, Bookbub, or Goodreads and say hello.

Made in United States
Troutdale, OR
01/15/2024